The War, Love, & Harmony Series: Book 5
# The Sheik's Blackmailed Bride

## Elizabeth Lennox

Note: Books 1 and 2 in The War, Love, & Harmony Series are free e-books.
Learn more about the series or download the free books at ElizabethLennox.com.

# CONTENTS

# About the War, Love, and Harmony Series

This series encompasses two generations of love stories across the four fictional neighboring countries of Larcatia, Altair, Lurasa, and Tularia. When the four betrothed princes and princesses fall in love with the wrong partner, a devastating chain of events is set into motion. Only the future leaders can put things right.

The first two stories tell the tales of two princes and their unplanned romances. These books are available free as e-books from ElizabethLennox.com.

*Fighting with the Infuriating Prince*: Jalayla couldn't believe the arrogance of the man! To actually order her around? How rude! But beneath the surface of her anger towards the handsome prince, there was a simmering heat, an uninvited fascination with the man that she couldn't seem to fight. Every time he touched her, every time he even looked at her, she felt that strange sensation.

Tasir wanted to fire her at first sight. She argued with him about everything and challenged him in ways that no other woman dared. So why did he want to pick the woman up and make love to her? Initially, he didn't know that the lovely woman with fiery eyes and a sensuous figure was the one and only Princess Jalayla. And was determined that he would have her for his own.

So what's a man to do when he finds out that the woman of his dreams is promised to marry another man?

*Dancing with the Dangerous Prince*: Jalayla couldn't believe the arrogance of the man! To actually order her around? How rude! But beneath the surface of her anger towards the handsome prince, there was a simmering heat, an uninvited fascination with the man that she

1

couldn't seem to fight. Every time he touched her, every time he even looked at her, she felt that strange sensation.

Tasir wanted to fire her at first sight. She argued with him about everything and challenged him in ways that no other woman dared. So why did he want to pick the woman up and make love to her? Initially, he didn't know that the lovely woman with fiery eyes and a sensuous figure was the one and only Princess Jalayla. And was determined that he would have her for his own.

So what's a man to do when he finds out that the woman of his dreams is promised to marry another man?

Two weddings! Two love matches that weren't supposed to be! Princess Ciara of Altair, previously engaged to Prince Tasir went on to marry Prince Zoran of Larcatia. While Prince Tasir of Lurasa weds Princess Jalayla of Tularia.

Unfortunately, the weddings don't result in peace. The two couples were able to experience only a short-lived interlude of calm before tensions escalated to the point that violence was inevitable. Even after the weddings and despite years of trying to calm the problems, the four countries break out into war. A ten year, brutal war that was never supposed to be.

Sheik Zahir del Hassar Alzar of Larcatia brings the three other ruling sheiks to the Fortress of the Guards in secret. These four men – some recently risen to their power, others who have been rulers for a few years – all agree that it is time to stop the war caused by the tensions that were started when their parents or ancestors married years ago. The fighting has been going on too long and nothing has been gained. Borders remain as they were before the wars took place and the reasons for fighting don't seem to apply any longer. The broken marriage contracts never should have resulted in war; peace must be restored for the benefit of all four countries.

After long and challenging negotiations, the four rulers agree to cease hostilities and sign treaties so that the healing process can begin. They devise a strategy to help their people diffuse the rivalries and tensions that have developed. The four men agree that the best way to show their subjects that life should move on, without war, is to each marry and produce an heir. Royal weddings and the birth of a new generation will give the people a reason to hope.

The saga continues with another generation, where the now-current rulers of Larcatia, Altair, Lurasa, and Tularia must fulfill their treaty obligations.

***The Sheik's Secret Bride***: Their story began five years ago. Callie fell madly, crazily in love with Zahir. But the war in his country was raging and nurturing their relationship was tenuous at best. When Callie was captured, the experience was terrifying. Zahir found and rescued her, but he knew it would be impossible to insulate her from danger in his country. Despite his wishes to be together, he knew that to keep her safe he must send her away. However, he wouldn't let her go until she was his bride. In a secret wedding, he married her, and then spirited her to safety.

She arrived in her haven traumatized, fearful, homeless…and pregnant. Slowly, she rebuilt her life, gave birth to her son and somehow learned to get on with living without Zahir. For five long years, Callie recovered from the nightmare of her captivity. And she raises her son.

When Zahir enters her life once more, she can't believe that the fire between them is hotter than before. But she refuses to give in, despite its intensity. She's too afraid that the peace between the previously warring countries will end and that she or her son could be in peril again. She yearns to feel safe, but can she defy her heart or deny her son his father?

***The Sheik's Angry Bride***: Duty. Responsibility. Those were the priorities of Layla's upbringing. So when her father announced that she is to marry the Sheik of Lurasa, she accepted her duty and steeled her heart to a loveless life of obligation.

What she refused to accept was Garon's intense effect on her. The man wasn't what she anticipated! And he wouldn't conform to her plans or expectations. This was an arranged marriage! They had appearances to maintain, duties to adhere to. Why were these crazy feelings flying between them every time he touched her?

Garon entered into the marriage expecting only to be faithful to his wife and to the agreement he had made with the other sheiks. What he wasn't expecting was a fiery beauty that set his senses on fire or the intense need to have her. Responsibility be damned, this woman was his! And he was going to teach her about living and loving.

*The Sheik's Blackmailed Bride*: Luna couldn't believe the chain of events that had led to her wedding day. All she'd wanted was to save her small village, to help the residents to get out from underneath their crippling debt. So she'd written to the man who owned the bank. And here she was, walking down the aisle toward a man she barely knew. A man who could make her body sing but who could crush her hopes and dreams with a few harsh words.

Dassar needed a wife. The lovely Luna fit none of his criteria. She was too soft, too sweet and would be hurt by palace life. So why couldn't he forget her? Why could she get under his skin so easily? And why couldn't he simply walk away?

*The Sheik's Convenient Bride*: The only reason Kylie had come back to the palace was to prove to everyone that she was over Tarek. Her girlish infatuation was a thing of the past. So how did she end up dining with the sheik? And why was her body still vibrating when he kissed her? Why couldn't she simply put her infatuation in the past where it belonged?

Tarek took one look at the fascinating beauty and knew that Kylie was the woman he was going to have for his wife. He didn't want to marry, but the terms of the peace treaty were absolute. So if he had to do it, why not do it with the lovely, feisty and sexy woman that he couldn't get out of his mind?

*Note to readers: Although the books of the series are related by this shared backstory, each is an independent story in its own right. With the preceding context for reference, the books may be read out of order. Books 1 and 2 are free e-books and may be downloaded from ElizabethLennox.com.*

# Prologue

She felt the icy rain that seeped slowly underneath her jacket, but ignored the knife-like pain. Despite the dusk that was coming on fast, she knew that she was almost there. Luna could see the town just off in the distance. Pushing on, she shifted her feet slightly in her worn sneakers, trying to avoid the hole where her big toe was now hitting the rough pavement. The friction had even worn away what was left of her cheap, well-used sock.

Wiping the rain from her eyes, she blinked once, trying to focus on the road ahead. Then twice, her heart speeding up with excitement and relief. There…it looked like just a dim light, but she was pretty sure that was the small town. She could see the warmth of the lights through the rain, a welcoming beacon that lured her forward. Just a few more steps, she told herself. Surely her mother would be there!

Luna looked down at the envelope once more, checking the address. Since the town was so small, it took her only moments to find the small inn where her mother worked. But even after she found the address, she was hesitant to go inside.

She stood under an old oak tree for several moments, staring through the window at the group of people inside. All of them were laughing about something as two older ladies poured tea or coffee. It was almost like a scene from a Norman Rockwell painting, she thought. She didn't belong in that kind of a setting, she told herself, backing deeper into the shadows.

One of the ladies spotted her outside in the rain and jerked upright, her eyes wide with…fear? Luna cringed, not wanting the kind-looking woman to be afraid of her, but she probably looked pretty rough in her second hand, rain-drenched clothes. But as she peered through the rain and the dusk, the woman didn't seem to be afraid. No, not fear, surprise.

The elderly woman disappeared for a moment, then she was there again, standing in the open doorway beckoning Luna to come inside. "Goodness, dear. Come in! Come inside! You'll catch your death of a cold out there!"

Luna looked behind her, just to make sure that the woman was speaking to her and not to someone else. When she realized that she was the only one standing in

5

the rain under the debatable protection of the oak tree, she turned back to the woman who was still gesturing for her to come into her establishment. Walking into the warmth was almost painful after so many days out in the elements.

The lady tsked when she realized how wet Luna was. "Oh my, you're soaked clear through to the bone. Take off that jacket right now and I'll put it in the dryer for you, dear."

Before Luna could decide whether to obey or sprint back outside into the cold, her jacket was pulled off by an older man with a stooped back. He shuffled out of the room with the coat in question. Unfortunately for her half-frozen body, the missing layer only intensified the feeling of painful cold surrounding her.

"What's your name, dear?" one of the other ladies said.

Luna looked around, noticing that everyone in the room was watching and waiting. "Luna. Luna Montgomery," she said through lips that felt frozen from the cold. There was an agonizing silence following that announcement. When no one seemed to be able to respond, she continued with her explanation for her presence. "I'm looking for my mother, Jenny Montgomery. Do any of you know her?" Luna asked. She pulled out the well-worn letter, trying to ignore the places where it had torn at the folds because she'd opened it too often. "She sent me this letter, telling me where she was and that I should come."

Luna stared at the group hopefully, but after several moments of awkward silence, that hope died. Their eyes told her the truth and she fought hard to keep herself upright, to not let the desolation bring her down until she could safely get away, find a hiding place. She hadn't eaten for three days and she was bitterly cold. Her stomach no longer ached for food because there wasn't any, and she had no place to sleep other than an old, dilapidated barn she'd seen a few miles back down the road. But she had to find her mother. She knew, as soon as she found her, everything would be okay.

"If she isn't here…" she started, ready to walk back out the door.

Jeanie Summerland shook her head. "Honey, you need something to eat." Turning to another woman, "Debbie, go get some of that soup, okay? And something warm to drink."

A man stood up. "She needs dry clothes, Jeanie. What happened to that old suitcase that someone left?"

Jeanie's wrinkled finger touched her chin as she tried to remember. "Oh!" she said and shook her finger at the older man. "It's back in the storage shed. Good idea. The clothes might not fit right, but they're dry and warm."

Oscar nodded and moved off quickly to the back, disappearing just as the other man had with her coat.

Debbie came back with towels and an enormous bowl of soup. "Honey, come sit right here by the fire. Once you've finished this soup, you're getting right into a warm bath. I'll bet your bones are even cold, aren't they dear?"

Luna accepted the bowl and the towels gratefully, but she was still worried. "Do any of you know my mother? Do you know where she is?"

Jeanie shook her head and waved towards the soup once again. "Finish your soup, dear. You're too cold and I suspect you haven't eaten enough for the past several days and you need to get your strength back up."

Luna's trembling increased, but this time it wasn't because of the cold. Something was wrong. She could see it in the eyes of the others around her. She wasn't sure what was going on, but....

Luna ate her soup and forced herself to smile when another kind woman put a cup of steaming hot chocolate on the table beside her. "Thank you," she whispered. These people were so kind and she wasn't used to kindness. She was used to...well, she wasn't going back there, she told herself. She was going to find her mother. One way or another, they would be reunited.

"Where are you from?" the woman called Jeanie asked gently. "Can we call someone for you?"

Luna's hand started trembling so badly that the soup sloshed over the side of the bowl. Thankfully, it ended up on her jeans and not the floor. "I'm fine," she told the woman.

"How old are you, dear?"

"Eighteen," Luna lied. She was only fifteen, but she knew that if she admitted she was underage, these folks would call her father. She was not going back to that man. Under no circumstances would she go back!

Jeanie and Debbie both looked at each other, neither believing her. "Well, finish that soup and then we'll talk."

Luna didn't like the sound of that, but she was too hungry at the moment to care. She just had to find her mother. She knew that everything would be okay once she found her mother.

When she'd emptied the bowl, she handed it back to the kind woman and picked up her hot chocolate. "I really just need to find my mother," she said softly.

Jeanie and Debbie moved closer while the rest of the group moved out of the room. Jeanie took Luna's hands and Luna knew that this wasn't going to be good. "I'm so sorry dear. Your mother was here; she's gone."

Luna's eyes looked at the woman, not sure why she was talking like that. "Do you know where she is now? I'll just walk there. I can do it."

Debbie shook her head. "No dear. She's gone. She passed away last year."

Luna heard the words but they didn't mean anything. Her mother was dead? Impossible! She'd just spent the last four days walking from New York to this small town. She'd found the letters! She'd found where her mother had gone! It wasn't possible that she was dead!

"I found letters in my father's closet last week. Those letters were from here. They said she was here. My mother was begging my father to let me come visit her. I'm here. I'm here to visit my mother."

Debbie's hand tightened on the frightened, young girl's hand that started trembling even more with the news. "If you're Luna, then yes, we know all about you, dear. Your mother talked about you all the time. She sent money to you. She worked so hard to pay for the lawyers so that she could get custody of you."

"She's not dead," Luna told them firmly. She refused to cry. Crying was bad. It solved nothing.

Jeanie and Debbie looked at each other sadly, not sure what to do.

Jeanie straightened up. "Honey, why don't we get you into a warm bath? I bet you could use a good night's sleep and then we'll tell you all about your mother in the morning. Would that be okay?" she asked tenderly.

Luna looked from one woman to the other, not sure what to do. In the end, she couldn't impose. These were kind ladies and if her mother was…

"I have to go," she said firmly. It was the only right thing to do.

Jeanie and Debbie both stood up along with the too-slender girl. "Dear, I would be very upset if you went out in this weather. Won't you please stay with us tonight?"

Debbie agreed. "We have this huge inn with ten empty rooms. It gets pretty lonely at night. And with the wind and rain, things sound…strange," she explained. "It would be really comforting if you could stay here with us. Another person in the house would feel much better."

Luna knew that these ladies were only trying to make her feel better, but she couldn't deny them their request. "Just one night," she whispered in agreement.

Jeanie clapped her hands and stood up. "Oh, thank you dear. Now, let me show you around."

Jeanie and Debbie took her on a tour of the inn, showing her the kitchen, the rooms and the storage areas. "If you need anything to eat, just grab something from here," Jeanie said. "We have plenty of food."

Luna smiled, her heart warming at the ladies' kindness.

An hour later, she was sitting in an old-fashioned bathtub, her body finally starting to warm up, when the door opened. Luna hugged her legs closer to her body, but the gasp came anyway. She couldn't hide her back, she realized.

But Jeanie quickly recovered and just set the fluffy bath towels down on the bench beside the tub. "Here you go, dear. Come on out when you're finished. Debbie just pulled an apple pie out of the oven. We're having it with ice cream tonight!" she said and disappeared back out the door.

Luna waited for several tense moments, wondering if the other woman was going to come back in. When there was just silence, Luna relaxed. Dipping into the water, she washed her hair, surprised at how much mud was caked on the almost-white strands. When she stood up, she took one of the towels, not bothering to look into the mirror. She knew what she'd see, and it wasn't pretty.

Luna emerged from the bathroom, wearing old sweatshirts and sweatpants that were about three sizes too big, but they were warm and comfortable, and with the warm socks, she felt slightly more human.

There was a pie just coming out of the oven when Luna walked into the warm kitchen. "Oh good, you're here!" Debbie said and put an extra-large piece of pie in front of Luna. "Now tell me what you know of your mother," Debbie said as the three of them dug into their dessert.

Luna gave the brief details of what she knew. She vaguely remembered warm, soft hands lifting her up and kissing her knee once. She remembered a song. But that's about it.

For the next hour, Debbie and Jeanie traded stories about her mother who had lived and worked in the inn for the past ten years. Debbie and Jeanie had basically adopted the woman and Luna felt sad that she couldn't remember her.

That night, after Debbie and Jeanie insisted on adding three additional blankets, Luna stared at the wall, letting the tears fall silently down into the pillow. Her mother was gone. She couldn't go back to her father. And she wasn't sure where she was going next.

With the beautiful child tucked into bed, Jeanie pulled Debbie aside. "That girl is covered with bruises, Debbie," she said angrily. "We need to call Don."

Debbie agreed. "He won't send her back, will he?"

Jeanie tapped her fingers against the countertop. "He won't. He'll protect her too."

Debbie nodded. "She's ours now," Debbie said firmly.

Jeanie agreed. "She's ours."

The two women were ready to take on the world for a bedraggled young girl they barely knew. All they understood was that this girl needed protection and they were going to give it.

A knock on the back door startled them but it was only Jim from down the street. "What are you doing out on a night like this?" Debbie said, pulling the younger man into the kitchen.

Jim was holding a big bag which he dumped onto the floor. "I heard that you had a young girl. Is she really Jenny's girl?" he asked.

Debbie and Jeanie nodded. "Yes. Poor child."

Jim sighed. "That's just tragic. But here are some of Diane's clothes. They're still probably too big for her. Norman said she was a little thing, but some of them might work."

Another knock on the kitchen sounded. Oscar just pushed his way in. "Is it really Jenny's girl?" he asked, his arthritic knees struggling to get up the one stair to the kitchen. Jim put out a hand to steady the older man and closed the door so the rain wouldn't come inside.

"Yes. And she's a mess."

"Here," the man said, pushing an old army coat and wool cap onto the countertop. "She can't wear that old coat she was wearing. This will be warmer." The man's bushy, white eyebrows came down lower. "Don't you let her go roaming around anymore, right?"

Jeanie shook her head. "She's not going anywhere. We'll take care of her."

Another knock sounded and this time, three of the mothers in the town walked in. "Is it Jenny's girl?" the leader asked. One woman was carrying a pot that was still too hot so she needed potholders. Another was carrying a loaf of bread that was still warm and wrapped in towels and the third set a cake carrier onto the counter. "She's not leaving, right?" the third one asked.

The kitchen was crowded with people trying to get reassurance that the young girl wouldn't be leaving any time soon.

Another knock. Another entrance, this time a big man in a sheriff's uniform walked into the kitchen. "So," he said and everyone in the room tensed for a brief moment. "You have your niece staying with you for a while?" he asked. Everyone relaxed. They should have known better. Don was a good man and a father himself. He knew the law. And he knew the right thing to do.

"Yes. Her name is Luna and she's going to be staying with us indefinitely."

Don nodded his head. "Good. You're going to need to get her into school. We'll figure that out. She can't drop out of school."

Everyone in the room nodded their head.

"She's our girl now," Debbie and Jeanie said, looking around at the others in the room.

"We're all going to help," Oscar said. "You can't keep Jenny's girl all to yourself."

Jeanie and Debbie smiled. "No. No more keeping Jenny's girl away. She's going to be fine. We owe it to Jenny."

Everyone agreed. And for the next four hours, they all came up with a plan.

# Chapter 1

"Have you contacted Faris and put my proposal to her?" Sheik Dassar bin Sarook asked, his eyes snapping while he walked to his next meeting. Faris was his current mistress, a beautiful woman who would be an adequate wife. He wasn't sure about mother, but he could always hire someone to act as nanny after children were born.

Hasif, the sheik's harried chief advisor, hustled to keep up with his employer's longer stride. Hasif was shorter by a foot and severely overweight, but he was a brilliant man when it came to details, allowing Dassar to focus on the bigger picture for Altair. After the seemingly relentless ten-year war, there was so much to do in order to bring prosperity back to Altair, and Dassar was not going to make his people suffer any more than they had to. Already, the economy was starting to come back to life and people were becoming more secure in their future.

The peace treaty with his former adversaries was a good one and Dassar was determined to put the final requirements into place as quickly as possible. Marry and secure succession with an heir. That was the plan for all four of them and Dassar wanted to finalize that issue as quickly as possible so his people knew what to expect. He knew that both Zahir and Garon had found women that were both beautiful and generous of spirit. He didn't think he would be that lucky and just wanted to find a wife that would fulfill the role. Someone outside of Altair and the other three countries so that the possibility of war breaking out wouldn't happen again.

"If I might be so bold," Hasif put in, huffing a bit as they rounded the corner of the palace. "Perhaps there might be a better answer to the need than the lovely Faris." Hasif had to bite the side of his lip to keep himself from cringing as he said the next words about the most selfish woman he'd ever met in his life. "I know she would be eminently eligible for the role of your wife, but I'm just putting an idea out there that perhaps there might be a better solution."

Dassar stopped and looked down at his advisor, causing the man to almost run into him with the unexpected stop. "Better solution? Faris is beautiful and composed, exactly what Altair needs." And he wouldn't fall in love with her, he thought. Exactly what *he* needed for a queen.

Hasif took pains to keep his expression blank. Any sort of disagreement might push this hard and tough man to do the opposite. "I agree, Your Highness," he replied, treading carefully since they were speaking about the man's current mistress. But Dassar went through women like some men changed ties. It wasn't that he was promiscuous, although he certainly had a way with the ladies. Charm and harsh good looks, not to mention extreme wealth and absolute power in his country were potent aphrodisiacs. The women flocked to him. Just by raising his finger, women almost ran to him, eager to warm his bed.

Hasif would admit that the woman in question was indeed lovely, but Faris was also cold and self-centered. She was spiteful to the palace staff and more intent on spending as much of her lover's massive wealth as she possibly could. When she wasn't catering to Dassar's every need in the bedroom, she was barking orders at the palace staff, interfering with Altair policy and being one of the most demanding, rude, inconsiderate women Hasif had ever had the misfortune to endure. The only break from this treatment was when the woman flew in Dassar's personal jet to one of the clothing capitals of the world to spend his money.

Hasif had worked hard to come up with an alternative for Dassar's marriage problem, and he hoped he'd found a good solution.

"Although Faris is indeed lovely, I'm not sure that she would be accepted by your people with open arms." He said that carefully, not sure how close Dassar was to the woman. If history had repeated itself, the lovely and evil Faris should have been on her way out the door a month ago. Hasif suspected that the only reason Dassar hadn't grown bored with her was because of the mutual agreement with the other three countries for each of their leaders to marry quickly and produce that heir. Since two of those rulers were already happily married, the pressure was on to do the same in Altair.

Hasif suspected that Faris knew about the marriage requirement as well, which was why she was so confident about her current role. And also why she'd become extra demanding lately.

The woman was pure evil, Hasif thought. It was imperative that Dassar find a woman with a heart inside of her chest and not just a cash register. After all the years of war, all the sacrifices his ruler made in order to protect the interests of Altair, Dassar deserved someone who would love him with all of her heart. Hasif was of the opinion that Faris, no matter how lovely she might be, could only love herself and the things she could earn from her time in Dassar's bed. And Hasif seriously doubted that Faris would trouble herself to bear Dassar an heir. The woman would manipulate events so that her outstanding figure remained intact – not destroyed by the potential ravages of pregnancy and birth.

And so he'd come up with another option.

"Why do you think she won't be accepted?" Dassar demanded, irritated that the issue had not been resolved already. He had too many things to do with his time; worrying about his marriage was not something he wanted to waste any time on.

Again, Hasif chose his words carefully. "She might be a bit harsh until one gets to know her softer side," Hasif said carefully, not mentioning that there wasn't a softer side to that horrible woman. "But I have another option. I have a woman who might be a better fit for this role. Someone a bit more docile and who…"

"Who is she?" Dassar demanded. If Hasif was doubtful that Faris could fulfill the role of his queen, then there was a legitimate reason for caution and looking at other possible candidates.

Hasif handed Dassar a file. "Read through this information, Your Highness. I think that this woman might be a perfect option."

Dassar took the file but didn't open it. "Fine. I'll read through it later. What's going on with the refinery in the south?" he asked, moving again towards his next meeting. And just that quickly, his marriage was pushed aside so that he could concentrate on more important issues.

The next meeting was just as tedious as the previous one and Dassar grew impatient with the arguing over the oil revenue. "Enough!" he called out. He opened the file in front of him, thinking that it was the file that contained the list of options for the refinery. But instead, his eyes were captured by a set of startling blue eyes surrounded by a cloud of platinum-blond hair. The lighting caused the blond tresses to look almost white and sharpened the contrast to the blue eyes. Her skin was pale with rosy cheeks, bringing to mind the image of a soft, English rose with blush colors and a pale center.

His eyes skimmed through the information, quickly absorbing the details. Hasif had done an excellent job of gathering intel on the woman and Dassar couldn't deny that he was intrigued. His initial reaction was to reject the idea. This woman, Dassar looked at the top of the page for her name, this Luna Montgomery, was too soft, too tender. She'd never make it in this world. Altair was a beautiful country and in another ten years, he would ensure that it was peaceful and economically stable. But the war had destroyed a great deal of the country's infrastructure. It was a difficult life here and there was a great deal to rebuild. Palace politics and intrigue alone could do in the average woman with a sensitive heart.

This Luna woman was only twenty-four years old. Not old enough, he thought and flipped the page. Reading through the letter she'd sent, he shook his head. She was pleading with him for a six-month reprieve for her little town in Central Virginia. Apparently, the recent recession had hurt the shopkeepers and most, if not all of them, were unable to make payments on their loans, loans which he owned since he owned the bank as well. He had to give her credit though. Not many people had figured out that he was the owner of that particular bank. It wasn't as if he kept it a secret, but it wasn't advertised either.

She herself owned the ten-room inn and, although she'd kept up with her loan payments, he read between the lines and knew that she was having a hard time as well. He flipped to the next page and, sure enough, a report on her financials was right there. Hasif was thorough. Dassar once again had to give his chief advisor credit for knowing all of the details Dassar would require for his plan to work.

He flipped through some other pages, reading about her volunteer work, the animals she kept as pets and even the herbs she grew in her garden which were used in the recipes she baked for her small bed and breakfast inn. The woman was creative and had grown her business over the years. Unfortunately, she'd extensively renovated and expanded her inn's kitchen right before the recession hit. Although the economy was coming back and guests were starting to patronize her business once again, they weren't coming back fast enough for her to keep up with the hefty payment schedule.

She was beautiful, he thought, his thumb rubbing along the picture as if it were actually her skin.

But not for him, he thought and snapped the file closed. Looking up at the men waiting expectantly at the conference room table, he nodded, pretending that he hadn't just completely lost the thread of the conversation while reading through a profile on a stunningly beautiful woman. Clearing his head of the crazy idea of making such a soft, lovely and gentle woman his bride, he abruptly said, "Send me the list and we'll break down the top five." With that, he walked out of the conference room, holding onto both the file as well as the list of priorities for the revenues discussed in that meeting.

"Set up a meeting," he told Hasif, tucking the file underneath his arm. That statement in itself was surprising since he'd just rejected the idea because the woman seemed too soft and delicate. But his next words shocked even himself. "We'll fly out this weekend to finalize the issue. Ensure that extra guards are brought up to my training standards so that she has adequate protection after the wedding."

With that, Dassar moved on to the next issue on his day's agenda, once again pushing the issue of his impending nuptials out of his mind.

He was oblivious to the glee that briefly shone on his chief advisor's normally bland features with the dramatic decision.

Hasif moved off in the opposite direction, eager to tell the palace staff to pack up Faris' belongings. He was going to tell her as soon as he could find her that the sheik no longer had need of her services.

# Chapter 2

"It isn't going to work," Barry said, handing her a bag of chicken feed.

"Of course it's going to work," Luna replied, accepting the bag and lugging it over her shoulder out of the shed. "The man isn't going to shut down the entire town."

"No, but he's probably going to sell off the assets so he can recoup his money." Barry walked behind her, wishing the Lovely Luna, as he referred to her in his mind, would let him do the heavy lifting for her. She was too slender, too slight of build to be lugging around those forty-pound bags of chicken feed.

Barry watched, unaware of the devotion that was shining through his eyes as he watched Luna spread the chicken feed out across the yard. She was sweet and wonderful and if she would only come out to dinner with him, he was sure he could prove to her that they could make it work.

"The whole town is gathering tonight to discuss the issue. It just doesn't make sense that he would evict an entire town, Barry." Luna bit her lip, hoping that her thinking was on target. She'd argued with everyone at last month's town meeting, telling them to at least give her plan a chance. Now she just had to prove that there was good in the world. She had to prove that this sheik guy was more than just a leader of a war-torn country. She knew that, deep down inside, everyone had a heart. Sometimes, it was just buried too deeply for a person to recognize that heart. This town had shown her that. Every person around this small town had taken her in and given her shelter in one way or another when she'd arrived here nine years ago. Ms. Prescott helped her catch up on all the math she'd missed, Barry's father had helped her with her readings skills, which were severely lacking because...well, because she'd fallen far behind in school back in New York.

Even her place here at the inn was because of the two ladies who had basically adopted her, watched over her, helped her heal. She'd come to this town broken and every person around had helped her to heal. So she wasn't going to give in until she gave back to them a little of what they'd done for her. She'd lost hope when she'd heard that her mother was gone. They'd given her a home, food, clothing and, most of all, hope. Hope in the goodness of the world.

The bank manager had already rejected her request. But she'd gone above him, only to be turned down by the odiously rude bank director. Never one to give up, she'd discovered that some sheik guy from that crazy country that had been at war for the past ten years actually owned the bank. So she'd tried one more time. So far, she hadn't received a rejection, so Luna was hopeful that there might be good news soon. No news meant no rejection, so she wasn't giving up hope.

"I don't have time to worry about it today though. Tonight is soon enough. I have a full house over the next few days," she told him. Turning to smile at Barry, she poured the rest of the bag of feed into the container, which would keep the chickens out but make tomorrow's feeding a bit easier. "And I'll make sure to encourage everyone to make their way to your art studio. Okay? See?" she said as she locked the bin and headed towards the kitchens again. "Everything is going to work out. A full house, lots of baked goods to sell, great art in your windows and even Mary Ann has doubled her chocolate goods for the weekend. Even she's optimistic that it will all work out. So why are you worrying?"

Barry shook his head as he watched Luna take off her boots, placing them carefully by the kitchen doorway. "You're just not realistic about how business works, Luna. I mean, why would the guy give us another chance?'

Luna was trying very hard not to lose patience with Barry's doom and gloom attitude, but it was growing tiresome. The man really was a worry-wart. Things worked out. They always worked out! She was living proof that things worked out when goodness and kindness prevailed. "Why wouldn't he? He's a businessman, right?"

"That is correct," a deep voice said from the kitchen doorway.

Luna spun around, a smile of greeting on her face. Which immediately froze when she caught sight of the man. He wasn't so much as standing in her doorway as overwhelming that limited space with his enormous size! She'd never seen a man as large and muscular as this man. Or as overtly terrifying either!

"Oh wow!" she whispered, taking in the tall, gorgeous man with shoulders that stretched across the expanse of the doorway. He actually had to duck as he walked into the room so that his head wouldn't smack into the top. And those eyes! Goodness, she looked up into those eyes and felt her heart beat faster. They were dark and mysterious and something just shot right through her. She could lose herself in those eyes, she thought.

Something nudged her arm but she didn't think anything of it, too amazed at the male specimen walking closer to her. But when Barry nudged her harder, she swung around to glare at him. Barry, in turn, looked at her pointedly.

Guests! "Oh! Right!" she gasped and snapped back to attention. "Right. Welcome!" she gushed. "I'm Luna Montgomery and welcome to the Moonside Inn," she told him. "Do you have reservations?" She gasped, "Oh, no! I hope you have reservations because otherwise, I might have to…" she shook her head. "No. I'm sure that everyone won't show up. We'll figure something out."

"We have reservations," the man standing in front of her said smoothly.

Dassar looked down at the blond woman and thought she was even more lovely in person. He hadn't thought that reality could live up to that picture of her smiling into the sunshine, but he had been wrong. This woman with her bright, blue eyes and platinum hair, she was simply beautiful. Her cheeks were the perfect color of a pink rose, a color which was only enhanced when she realized she'd been staring at him.

"Yes. Right!" she said again, receiving yet another nudge from Barry. "Stop that," she whispered furiously and stepped out of Barry's range so he couldn't nudge her again. "Anyway," she said, smiling up at the man. He really was amazingly attractive. That thin nose didn't detract from his looks in any way, she thought. And his hard jawline only made him look tougher in some way. Not at all like a male model. In fact, those pretty boys couldn't even come close to this man's raw, masculine appeal. Yes, they could take lessons from this man on how to appear manly.

"Luna!"

Luna jumped and turned to glare at Barry once again. "What?" she hissed.

"Stop staring," he admonished openly, the jealousy he was feeling hard to hide. Even Barry knew that he couldn't compare to this behemoth in the masculinity department, so he was eager for his Lovely Luna to get down to business so that the man would get out of her kitchen.

"I wasn't…" she looked up at the man, then blushed as she noticed he was still standing there, waiting for her to greet him correctly. "Oh. Well, so I am," she said out loud. "Anyway, yes…right. You have reservations." She wiped her hands on her jeans, wishing she was wearing something prettier, nicer, to greet this man. Or at least shoes, she thought and padded in her socks. She'd taken her boots off by the kitchen doorway, not wanting to track mud through her nice, clean kitchen. "This way," she told him and tried to slip past him. But he was too big and she had to halt, her eyes glancing up at him once again. "I can't get by," she whispered, her pulse pounding in her chest as her knees started to wobble. And it was all this man's fault!

Dassar looked down at the lovely woman, amusement shining out of his eyes. She was delightful, he thought. So innocent and naïve. Every thought was right there in her eyes and those blushes gave away her emotions too easily. No, this was not a good idea, he told himself. So why was he shifting slightly, giving her room to move into the receiving area of the inn?

She hesitated because he hadn't moved enough. And he should be a gentleman and give her more space, but he wanted to feel her softness just once before he left.

She smelled good, he realized as she squeezed by him in the close confines of the kitchen doorway. She smelled like fresh air and…lemons.

Luna tried very hard not to touch this man, but it was impossible not to feel the hard power under her fingers as she slipped by him, her hands automatically shifting out to balance herself as she moved past him. "If you'll follow me, I'll get…" she looked around, startled by the large group of men standing in her receiving area. They all wore serious expressions, all were dressed in dark suits, although none looked as perfectly tailored as the tall man's suit, but they all looked very…manly.

"Right, I'll just get everyone checked in. You're under one reservation?" she asked, not sure what was going on. She was getting a dangerous vibe and wasn't sure what to make of it. Normally she trusted her instincts even though they'd led her astray on some occasions.

But in this instance, with the tall, sexy man right behind her, she was too flustered to listen to her instincts. She was actually too flustered to hold the pen she tried to pick up, but she finally managed to wrap her fingers around the pen, only to realize that she needed to check everyone in through the computer on the front desk. Dropping the pen, she pressed several buttons. It took her a few painful moments because her fingers had suddenly turned into all thumbs and she'd double hit one key and completely missed the key she was aiming for. It was all terribly embarrassing since normally, she was quite efficient. It was only because the enormous man was crowding her, standing so closely behind her that she could actually feel the heat of his body through the sweatshirt she was wearing. And she had absolutely no idea how to politely ask him to move away.

She pulled up the information for this weekend's guest reservations. "Um…Mr. Smith?" she asked, looking up.

A short, chubby man with merry eyes and a ready smile stepped forward. "That would be all of us. I made the reservation under that name to protect our identities."

Luna blinked, not sure what to make of that statement. "Okay. Well, I can keep a secret," she told the man. "Did you want to…" she thought quickly. Then smiled. "I'm sorry, but this is a bit clandestine. Normally people who want to hide their identities are trying to…" she looked around, about to make a teasing joke about how people come to hotels under the name "Smith" in order to have affairs. But as she took in the stern, intimidating expressions on each of the men's faces, she thought better of it. "Never mind," she told the man. Pressing a few more buttons. "I just need a credit card to cover incidentals," she told him. "And you've booked all ten rooms, is that correct?"

"That's correct," the man said, handing her a credit card under the name John Smith.

Luna looked at the card, immediately becoming suspicious. But she rang the card through and, sure enough, it came up as clear. Since all of the rooms had been paid for in advance, she wasn't sure what to say. "Okay then, here are the keys," she said, looking around. "Do you know who will be staying in each of the rooms?"

"We'll sort it out," he said. "Which is the best room?" he asked.

Luna blinked, berating herself for not pointing that out before she'd handed the man all of the keys. Her only excuse was that she was too flustered with the gorgeous guy behind her. She could feel his eyes on her, suspected that he knew she was wearing her Bugs Bunny underwear and wished she'd worn her black lace. But those things itched and Bugs was more fun.

Ugh! Concentrate, she told herself.

Her fingers shook as she pulled the appropriate key out of the stack. "This is the King's room," she explained. "It has a beautiful four poster bed, a fireplace and a separate sitting room. It's really lovely." She went on to explain the other rooms and their advantages and locations before the man bowed and stepped back.

"You have been very helpful."

She smiled gratefully. Breathing a sigh of relief that the check in process was finally over. "Dinner will be served starting at six o'clock across the street. There is a bar over to your left if you'd like drinks or coffee, tea, hot chocolate," she finished that one, feeling silly for saying that. These men definitely didn't drink hot chocolate. And she was pretty sure that none would enjoy the marshmallows that she kept on hand for anyone who really did like hot chocolate. She might be the only one in the room right now who would partake of that particular treat.

Taking a deep breath, she fought to keep her voice positive even though she'd very much like to duck under the front desk and wait until the big guy behind her had decided to move away and torment his next victim with his brooding x-ray vision. "Breakfast will be served tomorrow morning from seven until eleven and there are cookies and scones for an afternoon treat." She smiled brightly, feeling better now that she was on firmer territory. Who didn't like cookies and scones? Everyone loved them!

She brightened her smile, trying to appear professional and polite, despite her wobbly knees. "And if there is anything that you need, please don't hesitate to call me."

The men disappeared, some going upstairs swiftly, others moving towards the back of the inn and several more moved outside. She saw the outside men fan out and it looked suspiciously like they were looking for criminals. In her yard? The worst they might find was Dorothy, her lazy hound dog or Lucifer, the cat that came and went whenever he wanted food. This was a small town with only a few people living and working here. If one were to drive a couple of miles down the road, they would come to a bigger commercial area filled with all of the big box stores. But this town was small and they worked hard to keep it that way. There was an old-time feel to the shops that were enhanced by their location close to the various historical sites around the area.

It took less than three minutes for the room to clear out, but Luna knew that the man who had never been far from her mind was still behind her. Still staring at her butt. Darn it, she should have worn the black lace no matter how itchy they were.

"How long are you going to ignore me?" the man asked, amusement apparent in his deep voice.

Luna sighed and turned around, her hands clutching the front desk behind her for support. "I'm sorry. I wasn't trying to be rude. It's just that..." she wasn't sure what to say. "You are the sexiest thing that has ever crossed my path" just didn't seem like such a sophisticated thing to utter. This man looked like he ate monsters for breakfast, he was just that tough looking.

"Have a drink with me," he commanded and took her hand, leading her into the small sitting room. At one end of the room was a wooden bar, but it was closed since it was only eleven o'clock in the morning. But there was a coffee and tea service sitting out and she walked over to it, pouring him a cup of coffee. "How do you take it?" she asked, setting the delicate cup and saucer down on the tray table because the cup was clattering from her nervousness.

"You're nervous," he said and took the coffee urn, pouring her a cup and handing it to her. "Why?" he asked when they were both sitting down.

Luna didn't have the heart to tell him that she didn't drink coffee. She'd always found the taste too harsh. Bitter almost. So she set the cup on the small table beside her chair and rested her hands in her lap. "I'm sorry," she replied. "I don't know why I'm so nervous. It isn't like I haven't had men in the house before," she said, then stopped, looking across the small expanse at him, shocked at what she'd just said. "I mean...of course I haven't *been* with a man in the house..." her eyes closed and she shook her head. "I mean..." she wasn't sure what she meant any longer and when his laughter hit her, she just stopped talking.

When his laughter died down, he looked at her with amusement still shining through his dark eyes. "I suspect that I know what you mean, but I'm glad to hear that you don't normally carry on with men who stay at this beautiful inn. There must be ample opportunities for you to socialize though."

Luna breathed a sigh of relief, glad that he was letting her off the hook even though she was flubbing her lame attempt at sophisticated conversation. She simply wasn't a sophisticated kind of woman. She was just down to earth, what-you-see-is-what-you-get type of person. "No. Not really. The inn takes up a great deal of my time."

Dassar couldn't believe that this woman, with her silver hair and her bright, eager eyes with the slanting, cat-like glance, hadn't been propositioned by numerous men over the years. She was too beautiful, too enticing. "But the other guests who come to stay overnight, surely some have been interested."

She shook her head. "No. This is an out of the way location. Anyone coming here is staying for a romantic getaway with their significant other," she smiled. "So the men are mostly taken."

"Good to know. And what about your boyfriend?" he asked, probing mercilessly but unconcerned with how he was perceived. This was to be his wife, his queen and he wanted to know more about her. Everything was telling him that she wouldn't work out, that he should turn and walk away. He needed a woman who could be strong under pressure, who would be able to handle herself with him. He knew that he wasn't the easiest man to live with. But his wife would have to be faithful.

Luna shook her head. "I'm not seeing anyone," she said but not sure why she was admitting all of this to this stranger. She suddenly realized that she didn't even know his name. How could she have revealed so much to a stranger? But for some reason, he didn't feel like a stranger. As she looked into his dark eyes, she sensed that this tall, intimidating man was just as lonely in his high-pressure occupation as she was despite both of them being surrounded by people almost constantly.

How crazy was that, she thought? A man as gorgeous and sexy as this man couldn't possibly be lonely. But still....

"What about the man in the kitchen? The one who kept punching you."

Luna laughed, the idea of her and Barry as a couple was ludicrous. "Barry? Oh goodness, he's just a friend." She was watching the man under her lashes and thought she sensed a relaxing in his shoulders with her statement. But that was impossible.

"So you are the owner here," he stated with a change of subject. Dassar was satisfied that she was relatively innocent, although he suspected she wasn't a virgin. No woman who looked like she did and was as open and honest as she was could remain untouched. He didn't like it, but he definitely liked her. "Tell me what it is like to own a small inn like this?"

"Oh, the cleaning and early mornings are a bit of a problem for me, since I love sleeping in and I absolutely hate doing laundry." She smiled even as she crinkled up her nose at the confession. "But I love cooking, which compensates for the rest of the chores. Just wait until you try my scones. They're really amazing," she told him.

"I will anticipate that experience with relish," he replied. He was truly enchanted by her enthusiasm, but hated the idea of this woman cleaning. Looking down, he realized that her hands were red, obviously used to the harsh chemicals needed to freshen up a hotel room after guests had stayed overnight. He'd have to speak to Hasif about getting her some help. He didn't like the idea of this little woman with her soft, beautiful skin, having to clean up after guests.

No, he couldn't marry this woman, but he could definitely make her life easier, he thought.

He stood up, determined to find Hasif and tell him they could leave. "Perhaps you would be kind enough to have dinner with me tonight?" Those words surprised even him, but the look on the lovely woman's face told him that she was surprised as well.

Luna stood as well, preferring not to look up at him quite so much. But the man was so tall that even standing still caused her to have to tilt her head back. "I'm so sorry," she gushed sincerely. "But I already have a big meeting with some people tonight and I can't miss it."

Dassar bowed slightly. "Another time then," and he walked out of the room. She was wrong for him, he thought again as he ascended the stairs. But she was beautiful and she stirred something inside of him that he hadn't felt in a long time. Actually, never, he realized. There was lust, absolutely, but there was something more, something that he couldn't quite define because he wasn't familiar with the sensation.

Surely it wasn't protectiveness, he thought. No, that was ridiculous.

He went upstairs and spoke to Hasif about other matters, the issue of the lovely Luna spinning around in his mind. In the end, he shook his head.

"I can't marry the woman," he told his chief advisor.

Hasif had recognized the signs in this man. He was interested in the woman. More than interested. And from the small bit of interaction he'd witnessed, Luna Montgomery was exactly what this man, and Altair, needed. She would bring life and happiness to this man. She was filled with hope and optimism. She was perfect.

But he had to be careful.

"Perhaps you are right," he said and started gathering up the papers he and Dassar had been working on moments ago. "Another man might be better suited to marry her."

Hasif wasn't looking, but he could feel the rise in tension. After only a few minutes in the woman's company, Dassar was smitten. And his ruler certainly wouldn't like the idea of another man touching what Hasif suspected Dassar already considered his woman. Moments later, his suspicions were confirmed.

"This is a good place to relax and get some of the issues worked out," he announced. "So we will stay here for a few days and work on the details of that construction plan and the military bases."

Hasif didn't even crack a smile. He simply gathered up the papers and bowed out of the room. "Yes, Your Highness."

Two days later, Dassar walked into the small sitting room where his woman was setting out coffee and tea. She looked lovely and his body instantly reacted to her round bottom in the jeans. They weren't even tight jeans so why was his body reacting in this manner? He was frustrated that he hadn't been able to walk away from her, livid that he'd been talking to her each day, getting to know her and walking around with an erection almost every moment of his life lately. At night, he dreamed of making love to her and during the day, he couldn't tear his eyes away when she walked into the room.

It didn't help that she seemed to smile more brightly when he caught her attention or that her pale cheeks turned that lovely shade of pink. Their conversations consisted of mainly questions from him about her life, her hopes and dreams and he grudgingly admitted that he admired the woman. She was a good businesswoman but a bit too cautious, he thought. He offered her ideas on how to improve her inn and he enjoyed the way her eyes lit up at the possibilities he offered.

And he couldn't seem to walk away from her. Every time he spoke to her, he knew that she was the wrong kind of woman. But he couldn't seem to leave.

"Do you have time to take me on a tour of your inn?"

Luna thought about the sheets in the dryer and the cookie batter in the fridge. But the idea of spending a bit more time with this fascinating, enigmatic man was a bit too exciting to ignore. Every time he was near, she felt alive. He looked at her as if she were special and precious.

She felt like she was practically glowing at the idea of giving him a tour. He worked so hard, she loved the idea of showing him around outside, giving him a glance at the amazing mountains surrounding her little inn. "I would be happy to show you around."

He stood up and Luna was once again struck by his size. He really was an enormous man, she thought.

She felt awkward, and small! And somehow vulnerable. When he took her hand, she felt strange tingles travel throughout her whole body. Why didn't that happen when Barry touched her? Why did this mysterious man who was so completely out of her league, enthrall her as no other man ever had?

He didn't release it for several moments and Luna was struck by the shock of his touch, by the way her hands felt almost burned as their skin melded together. For the past couple of days, he'd always kept his distance, smiling at her, drawing her gaze to him like a magnet, but never once had he touched her even in a casual way.

She glanced up into his eyes, so surprised by her body's shocking reaction and wondering if he could feel it as well. It didn't make any sense, and this man's expression didn't give anything away.

Pulling her hand away from his warm grasp, she took a step back, trying to pull herself together. She was acting silly again, making more of a single instance than was real. She'd just imagined that heat, she told herself. It was ridiculous to imagine that one person's touch was warmer, or hotter, than another person's. All skin was basically the same.

So why was her hand still tingling even though they were no longer touching?

She sighed but then forced a smile to her face as the tall man lifted his hand to the doorway, indicating she should go out first. "This way," she told him.

She led him outside, thinking that the fresh air and openness might clear her head a bit more, put this man's presence into perspective. He was just a man, she told herself. Nothing different from Barry except, she stopped and looked back at the man's height and brawn...okay, so Barry needed to do about a thousand pushups and crunches to even start to come close to this man's muscular frame. And this guy had about six inches on Barry. Maybe eight or nine inches on her, she thought, standing up straighter in an effort to make herself appear taller than her five foot, six inch height.

"We have weddings out here by the gazebo," she explained, then blushed when she realized how silly that sounded. "Sorry," she mumbled. "You don't care about weddings, I'm sure."

"Not true," he countered. "Weddings are lovely and an important part of every society's culture. Understanding the ceremonies of certain cultures can tell a lot about what is important to a country."

Her smile brightened with his words and she relaxed her shoulders slightly. "That's so true," she replied. "I don't agree that the bride should be the princess though. I mean, it's the groom's day as well, right?"

He smiled at her words, a mysterious light coming into his eyes. "Ah, but it is the bride's time to shine. She becomes a princess on that day, does she not?"

Luna thought about that for a moment. "Well, only for a day."

His dark eyes looked down into her light, blue ones and thought about her in a flowing gown, walking towards him with a look in her eyes that promised him heaven. "For some women, it is only for a day," he replied, suspecting that his little lady had a very romantic nature. Her hair was reflecting the sunshine and it was startling in its beauty. And in that moment, he gave in to what he could now see what inevitable. Luna would be his wife, and more than a princess.

Luna felt that strange bubbliness rise up in her stomach again but tried to ignore it. This man was not for her and she needed to keep that uppermost in her mind. Focus on the work, she told him. Show him her inn and keep her role in perspective. She was just an innkeeper, she told herself. She washed linens, baked cookies and cleaned bathrooms for a living. While this man, she gazed up at him curiously through the haze of romantic glow that she couldn't seem to make go away, he was someone important. If she hadn't guessed it by his expensive clothes, she would have figured it out from the way he held himself. This man didn't speak "power", his very presence shouted it out to the world for him.

She showed him the pathway that she'd carefully cut into the woods, explaining the different plants in the region, the dangerous ones like poison ivy as well as the more interesting flowers like the red bud tree that flourished here in Virginia and, in the springtime, the flowers could be eaten as a sweet treat.

It wasn't all that interesting though since there weren't many leaves on the plants at the moment. But he could see the poison ivy vine and the remains of the roses. "And here," she said as she led him around the corner of the pathway, "is the main allure." She stopped and showed him the view of the mountains in the distance. Her wonderful, little village was nestled in the foothills of the Shenandoah Mountains and, from this vantage point, one could look out and see the many layers of the mountains through the distance in varying shades going from a murky green during the early springtime on the closer hills to the grayish blue of the mountain ranges beyond. On a day like today with the sun shining brightly, one could see for miles and it was an astounding sight.

"Beautiful," Dassar said, looking down at the woman with the pink cheeks and tousled hair. She was amazing, he thought. A woman who appeared kind and innocent, and he suspected her heart was the same. She was so unlike the women he'd taken to his bed in the past that it had just taken him a few days to get to know her properly to understand her value.

That was all this was, he told himself. This strange feeling he'd been having during every conversation, it had only been amazement that such a person existed.

He lifted her up and set her down on one of the rocks which lifted her up enough so that she was almost at eye level with him. "I'm going to kiss you, Luna," he told her, giving her fair warning.

Luna blushed an even deeper pink. "Oh, that would be very nice, but I don't think…"

She didn't have a chance to finish her argument because his hands on her waist pulled her forward. A moment later, his soft, gentle kiss struck her and she was no longer able to utter a word. She was stunned by the power of his tender kiss. When he lifted his head, her eyes opened up and she looked up at him, found him watching her carefully. And then he did it again, testing her lips, tasting them almost. When his hand moved from her waist to the back of her head, she sighed with happiness and allowed him to tilt her head so that the kiss could deepen.

What had started out as soft and gentle, changed. This was no longer exploratory and Luna clung to the man, shivering with shock and amazement…and a desire to deepen the kiss even more! And then she couldn't think any longer.

Instinct took over and all she could do was react to his kiss, to the way his kiss made her feel.

Gone was the tenderness and it was replaced by a kiss so powerful, so commanding, she was trembling in his arms, her hands moving from his arms so that they wrapped around his shoulders. Luna wasn't aware of anything except for the desire that pooled in her belly and then shot outward like a red-hot flare, sizzling in intensity and causing her to cling to him, pressing her body against his hard frame. The strange noises she vaguely heard were from her as she experienced desire for the first time in her life. At the hands of a man she'd only known for a couple of days, no less!

Dassar lifted his head and looked down at the woman. Her lips were swollen from his kisses and her eyes were still closed. She looked like she'd been thoroughly kissed and his body hardened even more. How could a woman with such blatant innocence tempt him to such an extent? He preferred women who were worldly, who knew what they wanted in bed and were explicit with their needs. He wanted a woman who could...

He wanted her.

Enough said.

Pulling back, he almost smiled when her eyes opened up and she blushed even more.

Luna jerked backwards, horrified that she'd just kissed a man that she'd known for such a short time. "That did not happen," she told him sternly, stepping down off of the rock with shaking knees.

Dassar thought she was adorable although he didn't like her denial. "It happened," he countered, holding her elbow as she almost stumbled on the rocks. "And it will happen again. Very soon."

She shook her head and tried to step away. "No. This did not happen." Luna was flustered and embarrassed at how she'd acted like a complete floozy! She'd never kissed a man like she'd kissed this stranger. A few fascinating conversations with him did not give her any knowledge of him as a human nor could she excuse her behavior by saying that the past two days made him less of a stranger.

And she'd never so lost her head that she'd been unaware of her surroundings. This wasn't her. This strange feeling she was experiencing, this fluttering, tightening deep down in her belly, well, that wasn't happening either! She simply was not the kind of woman who did things like this!

Dassar sighed and took her hand. "Perhaps I should introduce myself more thoroughly. "I am Dassar bin Sarook, Sheik of Altair. You contacted me about the loans you and your fellow shop owners took out with my bank. I believe you were asking for a loan extension for yourself and the other vendors within the town?"

Luna gasped, her hands coming up to her cheeks as the horror of what he was saying hit her. "I won't do it!" she snapped.

Dassar wasn't sure what she was talking about, but he didn't like her instantly saying no. No one said no to him. "Excuse me?" he replied in a tone that others would hear and understand that they should tread lightly. But not Luna.

"I won't do it! I will not sell my body for money! I'm not a prostitute and you can just…go to hell!"

With that, she turned and ran back down the pathway, ignoring his sharply spoken "Luna!" as she rounded the corner. She ran as fast as she could, wanting to put as much space between herself and the man as she could. She was so ashamed, she couldn't believe what she'd just done! Goodness, it was no wonder the man thought she might be willing to…she couldn't let him think that about her.

She rushed back to the inn and burst into the kitchen, feeling better now that she was surrounded by her stove and her large island where she could make just about anything her heart desired. The smooth, marble surface, a huge splurge during her renovation process, helped her spread her baking out, making her feel better and more in control.

She wiped the tears from her cheeks with her arm, angrily heading towards her pantry. Taking down flour and sugar and other ingredients, she just started mixing, not really sure what she was going to make. But it felt good to be doing something with her hands.

When the kitchen door burst open and the large male came through the door, she cringed. "You can't be in here," she told him. "Guests need to stay in the front rooms."

Dassar ignored her order, stepping closer to her. "Don't ever run away from me again," he told her with harsh finality.

She spun around, her blue eyes blazing with fury at his command. "You can't tell me what to do," she spat back at him. She wasn't sure what to do with all of this impotent fury that she felt towards this man who had just kissed her. "You really need to get out of my kitchen." She took a deep breath, trying to calm down her raging feelings and this horrible sensation of humiliation.

Dassar walked over to her and pulled her into his arms, furious with her for ignoring his commands. He'd meant to give her a set down, to tell her exactly how their relationship was going to work, where he gave a command and she followed the order without question. But he found himself kissing her instead. And when she resisted, he kissed her harder, not allowing her any space. She fought him for only a moment before she melted against him and participated in the kiss and all thoughts of reprimanding her for her anger, her daring and for running away flew out of his mind. His intention to subdue her was obliterated but then the pleasure of feeling her lips move against his obliterated everything else. He pulled her closer, needing to feel her soft breasts against his chest, to understand once more exactly how their bodies fit together.

Lifting his head, he enjoyed the way her body leaned against his and her forehead fell to his chest while she tried to get her breathing back under control.

"Don't ever run away from me again. Please." He added that last word when she stiffened in his arms and he knew that he'd made the right decision when she once again relaxed. Why he'd even bothered was beyond him. Normally, he gave commands and they were followed. Why he was adding extraneous words to his commands for this woman's overly sensitive nature was beyond him.

His hands moved up to her hair, running his fingers through her soft, platinum tresses and enjoying the way she sighed when he massaged the tense muscles at the base of her neck.

She must have realized what she was doing because, a moment later, she pulled out of his arms, looking down at her hands that were shaking now. "Please, I'll get fined by the health inspector if a guest is found in my kitchen. The health department frowns upon strangers in here."

Dassar knew that he needed to have a conversation with this woman, but he also suspected that she would need some time to recover from their tour. Or his kiss.

"We'll talk later. We have much to discuss," he told her. "There is a mutually beneficial arrangement that I will present to you. I want you to listen to it carefully and thoughtfully."

Luna was about to shake her head. She didn't want any 'mutually beneficial arrangement'. Just thinking the words made her feel sullied. But before she could say a word, he pressed a finger to her lips, stopping her rejection. "No, it isn't what you are thinking, Luna." He removed his finger and she saw the amusement in his eyes. "When you are finished in here, come to my suite and we will discuss the issue of your loan, and the loans of the other vendors around here. There is a solution. And you're going to trust me."

She was so relieved by his words "not what you think" that she actually laughed when he told her to trust him. "Right," she said, not able to hide her sarcasm but it was softened by the fact that she wasn't angry with him any longer. She was still angry with herself, but that was different.

He looked behind her at the metal bowl filled with…he had no idea what was in there. It looked like a mess of white and…other strange colors. So he didn't even speculate as to what she might be cooking. "How long do you need to finish this?" he asked her, noting her sarcasm but ignoring it. This time. He should probably admonish her for that, but she looked cute at the moment so he let it slide.

Luna exhaled and looked around. "I need an hour to finish this batch of cookies and then I'll need to start on the breakfast items. I don't need to bake everything, just get it ready." She bit her lip as she thought through all of the things she wanted to cook which effectively kept her mind from rehashing the kiss outside. The kiss which had almost spoiled the one area that always soothed her when she was having problems. Her kitchen was the one place to which she could retreat and kept her from trying to imagine what "mutually beneficial" topics this man might present to her that wouldn't insult her being.

"I know all of the men with you have big appetites." she commented with relish, wanting to lose herself in baking something exceptionally delicious and sinfully unhealthy. It was one of the biggest perks of this job, watching people enjoy her food. She loved to cook and loved it when people savored her breakfast meals. She made sure that all of her foods were decadent and over the top.

Dassar didn't understand the hopeful light in her eyes as she spoke. It seemed strange that she should become excited at the idea of large men eating her out of house and home. "They will be satisfied with anything that is served."

She knew that his men weren't picky eaters but she just smiled with keen anticipation. "Good. Then they'll be thrilled with what I have planned for tomorrow morning." She looked up at the ceiling, not wanting to look at him for fear of what she might see. "Give me a few hours, okay?" It suddenly occurred to her that this man might simply be trying to ease the payment schedule for their loans. Isn't that what she had written to him about, asking for an extension? The idea suddenly had huge appeal and soothed her ruffled temper. "And should I get the rest of the shop owners together? They'll probably want to work with you on the solution. They don't want a free pass. They just need a bit more time. All the businesses are coming back now that the recession is easing," she told him, her eyes wide with sincerity and a strong hope that she'd misinterpreted his statements earlier.

His hand lifted to dust some flower off of her shockingly soft skin. "No. This discussion is only between you and me. What you decide to tell the others, that's your business." Of course, they'd know eventually anyway, but he wasn't going to mention that part of his solution right now. He was determined to get her alone before he mentioned anything about his plan. And her future as his wife.

He left her then, making his way up to his room. He had been pleasantly surprised by the size of the room. It was bigger than he had anticipated and filled with old style warmth. The fire was already crackling today and he motioned for Hasif to come in so they could get more work done.

Several hours later, Dassar glanced at his watch. She should be finished, he thought. He wanted to order a bottle of wine, thinking the alcohol might soothe the conversation. But he wasn't sure if Luna was the only employee here. He certainly hoped not. He didn't like the idea of her making up all the beds, plus the cooking and cleaning and everything else that had to happen in an inn of this size.

"She is still down in the kitchen, Your Highness," Hasif told him.

Dassar scowled. "She needs to take a break," he snapped, standing up and pacing the room. "She is working too hard." He'd seen her small hands and the skin had been red, her nails chipped. She shouldn't be doing all of the work. She should hire someone to take on some of the jobs so that she could have a bit more down time, a bit of time for pampering. Didn't all women need several hours a day to make themselves feel better?

Of course, hiring additional workers would put her further in debt so he at least had to admire the woman for getting things done and trying to dig herself out of the problem. She was dedicated and hardworking, willing to do what it took to get the job accomplished and make her guests feel comfortable.

That didn't mean he was going to allow her to work herself into exhaustion for his security team though. "Get some pastries from another bakery for breakfast. She shouldn't have to feed our men. She should start acting like her future role."

"Yes, Your Highness," Hasif said and stepped out of the room to follow that order. He also moved down the stairs, wanting to check on the woman in question.

He found her standing in the kitchen talking with several strangers. He stopped and listened, not ashamed at all of eavesdropping. He considered it his job, no, his responsibility, to find out if there were any hidden problems with the woman he'd presented to his ruler. This woman was going to stand by a man who ruled a powerful country. There could be no secrets that could come out later and embarrass his sheik.

"No, I'm sorry, Nancy. I don't know what's going on. Nothing more has happened since the meeting the other night."

"Well who is he? He's been here a couple of days and his men have already bought up all the chocolate we made."

Luna had already mentioned the new information she'd just learned, that Dassar was actually a sheik, the very same sheik she'd written to for help. That little piece of information seemed to make everyone more nervous so here she was, trying to calm the small crowd down. "I just know that he works very hard and he seems…" she hesitated before she finished with, "nice. He doesn't seem like he's about to kick everyone out of their homes and businesses." At least she hoped that was the case. Surely he would have said something by now if he was going to get rid of everyone. Wouldn't he?

That "mutually beneficial" comment was starting to haunt her. Luna had no idea what the man might want. Other than the obvious, which Dassar said wasn't the case.

"But what about all the men he has with him?" Tom asked, the owner of the bookshop around the corner.

That was a good point, Luna thought. There were a lot of men, more than she'd anticipated. "I don't know what the men are for," she told him, thinking about how she'd seen them scouring through the woods earlier, possibly security? But the idea was strange. She'd never met anyone who needed security guards. Besides, there were too many of them for that. One or two maybe. "I'm sure they're all very kind gentlemen as well."

Hasif tried not to snort in surprise. The men she was speaking about would be offended to be described as kind. Their jobs were to be the exact opposite of kind. Personal guard to the Sheik of Altair was a position of intense responsibility and deep loyalty. They were the most highly trained men in the military and had to constantly pass muster in order to maintain their positions. They were brutal men, determined to protect their ruler against any threat. Every man on this detail would lay down his life in order to protect their ruler. Their loyalty as well as their intelligence and ability to snap into quick action in order to save their sheik's life was absolute.

The pretty, little woman had her hands full trying to calm down the townspeople, all of whom were laying the burden of their bad investments and financial decisions on her slender shoulders. Hasif didn't like what he was hearing, what she was having to endure.

"Listen everyone," she raised her hands, trying to calm their nervousness. "He's here, let's just listen to what he has to offer. I'm sure he didn't come all this way just to kick everyone out. He could have just had the bank manager do that for him."

Hasif had to agree with her on that part. The Sheik of Altair would not lower himself in details like the financial future of this small town. That would definitely be the task of someone lower in rank. Of course, if Ms. Montgomery….No. He wouldn't think that way. Every instinct inside of Hasif was telling him that this woman was the right person for the job. She was gentle and kind and obviously had garnered great respect from all of these people who were definitely older and should be reassuring her, and not the other way around. It boded well that she felt this sense of protection for these people. She would give that same protectiveness to the people of Altair once she got to know some of them.

Luna was distinctly aware of the large man upstairs that was waiting on her. She wasn't sure what he would think about her tardiness, but nor was she going to throw everyone out in order to meet with him. She wasn't that eager to be intimidated once again. "So how about if we all meet over at the coffee shop tonight? I'll find out what he's going to offer and will let all of you know as soon as I find out. Okay?"

Hasif heard the grumblings but what were the townspeople supposed to do? They didn't really have an alternative. Especially since Ms. Montgomery seemed to be the only one who was offering any sort of options. He heard them shuffle out through the kitchen doorway and peered inside. What he saw made his heart wrench. He was glad Dassar was not witnessing the worried expression on the lovely woman's beautiful features. He would not be happy.

Hasif thought carefully, wanting to make this marriage work. Dassar deserved a woman like Luna in his life. She was bright, intelligent and caring. And what's more, she seemed to be intensely attracted to Dassar. And Hasif had already witnessed how interested Dassar was in the lovely Luna. In fact, Hasif had never seen Dassar react to a woman like that before. It was fascinating, a bonus that will work to both of their benefits.

Luna went over to the kitchen sink and washed her hands. They weren't dirty, but it just felt better to have something to do rather than go upstairs to meet with that man.

He'd seemed so nice over the past couple of days. What had happened? How had her judgment been so off?

She excused herself for not knowing he was the Sheik of Altair. Who could have guessed that a man like that would come to their little village? It was crazy and she had no idea what he might offer her about the debts.

And that kiss! Goodness, how could she have succumbed so quickly to his kisses? She felt her cheeks turn pink just at the memory of how he had kissed her, the way her body had just melted into him, wanting more of whatever he might offer.

She turned around and looked at her kitchen. She'd had such wonderful plans for this room. How had her life gone so off course?

She took the dishtowel from the counter and wiped her hands with the soft cloth. And then, just for good measure, she wiped down her counters again, cleaning the marble island, adjusting the bowls on her shelves.

She was procrastinating, she told herself.

That's when she saw Mr. Smith standing in her kitchen doorway and she tried to stifle the startled cry. "I'm sorry," she said, her hand fluttering over her heart. "I didn't realize you were there."

Hasif bowed and stepped further into the warmth of the kitchen. "I was coming to see if you were ready to discuss options with His Highness."

Luna stared at the man, not sure who he was talking about. "Who?" she asked when the shorter man didn't appear to be going to say anything further.

"Sheik bin Sarook, ma'am," he explained, bowing for good measure. "I believe he is anticipating your arrival upstairs."

Luna sighed. "I don't want to talk to him," she whispered, her blue eyes pleading with the man to give her some sort of reprieve.

Hasif had no idea what to say to this woman. His mouth opened and closed, sure that he'd misunderstood. "He is waiting," was all he could utter. To ignore a summons by His Highness was unheard of. Hasif couldn't imagine any circumstance in which the sheik's orders would not be carried out in an expeditious manner.

Luna sighed, her shoulders sagging with the stress of meeting with a man she didn't understand and who...well, he terrified her! "Yes. I suppose he is."

Hasif watched the slender woman walk up the stairs, looking like she was walking to her execution. Surely it wasn't that bad, was it?

# Chapter 3

"Sit down, please," Dassar said and indicated the chair closest to the fire.

Luna nervously sat down, perched on the edge of the chair.

"You look like you're about to bolt out of here at the smallest enticement," he said with amusement as he sat down in the opposite chair.

Her mouth made a face and she looked down at her hands. "Well, I don't think we really run in the same circles. And I'm relatively sure I'm not going to like anything that you're going to offer. In fact, I'm painfully aware of how much power you have over me, over this whole village and I'm begging you to consider how many lives you hold in your hand and have some compassion."

Dassar ignored the second part, dismissing the idea that he had any compassion. He was not known for his compassion or his mercy. He was known for getting things accomplished. Which was what he was doing now. So instead, he focused on the first part of her statement. "You don't think that we are similar in tastes?" he asked.

She blew out her breath, unaware of how the expulsion made her platinum tresses dance around her beautiful face. "Preferences don't really have any relevance. You are a sheik. A ruler of a country. You have powers that I can't even comprehend. And I…well, I don't really have a whole lot of power. I'm a shopkeeper with a precarious bank balance, trying to make a life for myself and the people around me."

Dassar disagreed with her. "You don't think you have power over me?" he asked carefully, not wanting to give her a power she might not know she had over him. But he didn't like the vulnerable look in her eyes either.

"I don't think that we are alike."

He looked at her soft breasts and her slender waist. "I have to agree with you there," he said with a chuckle.

Her stomach tightened with the sexual undertones of his comment. Was he teasing her? She certainly hoped not. Luna was not in a teasing sort of mood. In fact, she wished he'd just come straight to the point, not leave her wondering about his intentions. "So what is this arrangement that you want from me?"

He looked at her carefully. "I need a wife. And an heir," he said, just to make sure they were very clear.

Luna swallowed, wondering why the idea of this man being married to another woman bothered her so much. He was an extremely handsome man and a powerful one at that. Surely women fell all over themselves to jump into the man's bed. She doubted very much that the man lived like a monk. "Well, that still doesn't explain what we are doing here. Alone. In this room."

He watched her carefully, his eyes assessing her mood as well as her willingness to fall in to his plans. "I want you to be my wife, Luna. I want you to bear my children. In return, I will absolve the debts on this inn as well as the outstanding balances on each of the shop owners in this town. All you have to do is say yes."

# Chapter 4

She was just pulling the last of the bread pudding out of the oven and Luna smiled as she breathed in the perfect smell. Vanilla, cinnamon, and soft, freshly baked bread was one of the best ways to wake up in the morning. "Oh, they are going to love this!" she said with an eager smile. All thoughts about marriage and babies and leaving this village were gone for the moment as she soothed her exhaustion with baking something warm and delicious. She hadn't slept at all last night, her mind too stunned by the "mutually beneficial" bargain that horrible man had offered to her.

"Knock knock!"

Luna set the bread pudding down on the counter to cool slightly before she added the icing and turned around, pulling her hands out of the oven mitts.

Unfortunately, the man who had just walked into her kitchen was not a welcome addition. "What are you doing here?" she demanded, the friendly smile falling away from her face as she watched Burt Lansdale stepped into her kitchen through the back door. Her eyes dropped to the large box filled with breads and pastries. Burt was the baker in the next town over and a jerk of epic proportions. He was always asking her out on dates, but the offers sounded like a filthy invitation to a whorehouse. She'd never accepted any of his invitations and the fact that he would dare to enter her kitchen, especially with baked goods, just sent her temper over the edge from which it had been teetering since the previous night. "And get rid of all that stuff!" she practically growled. "I don't need any of it."

Burt set the large box filled with freshly baked breads down on her countertop and chuckled. It was a vile, disgusting sound that sent shivers of revulsion throughout her body. "Ah, but that's not what I heard," he told her and his eyes traveled up and down her figure. "Looking good, my little woman. When are you going to give up this place and let me take care of you?" he asked, referring to his constant pressure for her to date him.

She cringed, thinking of his enormous belly that, even now, was covered with a messy apron. "Don't hold your breath. And get rid of that stuff."

Burt rubbed his hands across his protruding belly, as if the size of his gut was validation of his masculinity. "No can do, my lovely." He shoved the box further onto her countertop. "I received an order last night from some guy named John Smith. These breads and pastries are already paid for so here you go."

Luna's mouth dropped in disgust as she realized that the man who had kissed her, several times, and offered her marriage in such a callous, horrible manner, throwing her life into a crazy whirl of confusion and a strange, unfamiliar desire, had gone and ordered freshly baked breads from the enemy! "He didn't!" she gasped.

Burt laughed again. "He sure did. Must not like your cooking," he said, peering over her shoulder at the bread pudding. "But I sure do. Want me to take that off of your hands?" he asked, already stepping forward, ready to do just that.

"Get out!" she yelled, more hurt at the man who had ordered the breads than at Burt. He was just gross. She wouldn't let him get under her skin.

Burt put his hands on his hips, in a very jovial mood since he'd just fulfilled a big order and got to see Luna in the process. It was a double treat, in his mind. "Now, is that any way to talk to your rescuer?" he teased.

Luna grabbed the first weapon she could find, which just happened to be one of the rolls he'd brought in. "Get out!" she screamed, throwing the roll at him and pelting him in the head.

"Are you crazy?" he yelled back, ducking when she picked up another roll.

Luna was feeling decidedly irrational. And tired since she hadn't slept very well last night. And the sleep that she finally did manage to sneak was filled with sexual dreams with one man in particular. "Yes. And it's all because of obnoxious men who think that I'm…" she didn't finish that statement, too hurt to even say the words. Not after last night and her conversation with the worst of all of them.

Burt scuttled out the door with a furious glare and Luna was just about to close her eyes, try to get her temper back under control. Unfortunately, her target entered her domain at that moment, throwing off her efforts.

"Luna, what is going on?" Dassar demanded when he stepped into the kitchen.

She swung around, her eyes flaring as the man in question appeared. "You!" she growled and took another roll. "So you're not even going to try mine?" she snapped and threw the roll across the kitchen. "Fine!" she said, not even bothered by the fact that the man easily caught the roll. She just lifted another and threw it across, aiming for his head. "You don't have to eat mine! You can just try Burt's disgusting rolls!" and another one flew from her fist across the kitchen, aimed at his head. Roll after roll headed towards Dassar's head. What was worse, he caught each one of them easily and tossed it onto the island, stepping closer to her with each attempted pelting.

"What are you talking about?" he demanded, his eyes narrowing as he concentrated on moving forward while still avoiding her missiles.

"My rolls aren't good enough for you?" Another one sprang across the room. "Fine!" she said and grabbed another one, flinging it towards him. "You can have this man's rolls. He doesn't make them with any cinnamon. He uses unhealthy white flour. And they are boring!" another one went flying. "And they aren't even warm! You could have had warm rolls!" another one headed for his head but by this time, he was less than a foot away from her. "But you won't ever know the wondrous nature of my…"

He lifted her up and set her down on the counter with an "oomph!"

Dassar trapped her hands so she couldn't grab another piece of bread, pinning them to her sides as he looked down at her. "Now explain to me why you are angry!"

"I'm not angry!" she almost yelled back, trying to pull her hands out from his grip. But he was too strong and that made her even more furious. "Let me go!"

"Stop fighting me or you're going to hurt yourself."

That infuriated her even further. "Oh no! You don't get out of the responsibility of hurting me. These are your hands pinning me down. So if I'm hurt then it is your fault!" And she wrestled with his hands again, only to realize that she was powerless. His grip wasn't hurting her, but she was still completely trapped by his hands. "Let me go!" she demanded.

He couldn't help his reaction. Her cheeks were pink with her anger and she was wiggling against him. Besides, she just looked incredibly sexy like this. Never had a woman thrown anything at him. None would dare!

"I don't think I will," he replied, stifling his laughter. "Give me one good reason why I should."

"Because I need to beat you for being such an obnoxious, horrible, insensitive lummox!"

He threw back his head and laughed. "I've been called many things in my life, pretty lady, but never a clumsy person." He looked behind her at the stack of rolls she'd tried to pelt him with and shook his head. "Besides, I think I have proven my adeptness while avoiding your very tempting breads."

That only incited her anger again. "Those aren't mine!" she growled at him. "And if you weren't such a horrible, insensitive jerk, then you would have tried my baking before rejecting it! How could you do that? I tried very hard yesterday afternoon to come up with things that would be enticing and…" she stopped, fighting back the tears. She took a deep breath and closed her eyes, trying to fight back the tears. "You didn't even try my breakfast," she finally whispered.

Dassar was at last understanding. "You thought I had my staff order additional breads because I didn't like your food?" he asked, his hands loosening on her wrists.

When she nodded, he shook his head, his hands came up to cup her face. "I had Hasif order additional foods so that you didn't have to work so hard, Luna." He waited for her eyes to clear.

His explanation didn't make her feel any better. It only showed that he didn't trust her abilities as an inn keeper. And that hurt almost as much as his distrust of her baking capabilities. "But I love cooking," she explained fervently. Her head turned towards the stove. "I have a maple syrup bread pudding fresh out of the oven for you. But you're not going to try it. You'll just have to deal with the boring breads that you ordered from the disgusting baker down in the next town over." With that, she pushed him out of the way and jumped down off of the countertop, unaware of the dust covering her derriere.

She turned her back on him, slipping her oven mitts back on so she could check on the bread in the oven. "So why don't you just go out into the dining room and I'll bring out these boring breads? You can just have…." She looked around, feeling disgusted by the very idea of bringing Burt's food into her inn. "Well, you'll just have to wonder what you missed." She lifted the box of breads and started carrying them out to the breakfast room but she stopped. "No, these are not going to mar the perfection of my breakfast," she said and turned back to Dassar. "I'll just feed these to the chickens. And you." She ignored Dassar's uplifted eyebrows at her announced punishment as she dumped the box outside the kitchen doorway. "These are my breads," she said and lifted another tray out of the oven. There were several types of yeasty, warm rolls that were perfectly browned. She allowed Dassar to watch her as she loaded up another basket, then walked back out to the dining room to replace the almost empty one she'd brought out earlier. Several men were already there, filling their plates with eggs and bacon, sausage and the freshly made waffles that she'd brought in right before Burt had arrived with his substandard fare.

"You should try the praline sauce with the waffles, Marid," she told the man with an identical black suit that the others were wearing. "It's amazing."

When the man politely nodded and started pouring the sauce onto his waffles, she smiled and walked back into the kitchen.

Her smile disappeared when she saw Dassar still standing in the kitchen. He looked as if he was about to take a bite out of the bread pudding she'd just pulled out of the oven. "Stop right there!" she ordered and lifted a wooden spoon out of the canister that held all of her cooking utensils. "Don't you dare!"

She wasn't aware of the two guards who hurried into the kitchen. Or the look Dassar gave to both of them, silently warning them to halt.

The men didn't leave, not really sure what they should do under the circumstances. Yes, they were there to guard their ruler. But he was being threatened by a pretty blond holding a wooden spoon. Besides, this was the woman who had baked the cookies for all of them the night before so it was understandable that their loyalties were confused.

"You said your bread pudding was better than Burt's. So I was going to try it out and see if you were telling the truth."

He started to dip his fork into the casserole dish but, before he could even get a bite onto his fork, his knuckles were wrapped by a wooden spoon.

Dassar looked up. The pain in his knuckles was nothing but he honestly wasn't sure if he should laugh at the two guards standing, unsure, in the doorway as they looked at each other then back at his woman, or if he should explain to Luna, his future wife, that she was not allowed to assault the present ruler of Altair under any circumstances. This was a completely new situation.

He chose to address Luna first, still stunned by her simple attack. "Did you just hit me?" he asked.

Luna glared right back at him, refusing to be intimidated.

"Yes. You are not allowed to have any of that. Nor is Hasif."

He stifled the chuckle at her words. "And why is that?" No one had ever denied him anything. Ever!

"First of all, it needs icing," she told him and lifted the sugary concoction she'd whipped up earlier, letting it drizzle over the still-warm pudding. When she was done, she slipped her hands into the hot pads and lifted the casserole dish, carrying it out of the kitchen. "And secondly, because you didn't trust me with cooking breakfast. This is what you get for that lack of trust."

Dassar stared in disbelief as the little woman with the flour covered butt walked out of the kitchen with the dessert-like breakfast food in her hands. She didn't even look back! She didn't care that he was ruler of one of the wealthiest countries in the world or that she'd just struck him, a crime that could be punishable by death or a life in prison, if he were to condemn her. Didn't she realize that he held the power of her business, of her village, in his hands? With the stroke of a pen, he could write off the whole village, let the bulldozers come in and demolish everything!

He looked towards his guards, both of whom were looking at his future wife, then back at him, silently asking for direction.

"I'll handle this," he told his guards with grim determination.

He couldn't let this insult to his person slide, he told himself as he leaned against the counter for Luna to come back into the kitchen. No, this was a moral imperative. He had to prove who was in charge here. The hitting, not to mention disallowing him to taste that incredible smelling concoction, had to be punished. And he was just the man to do it!

When her saucy little body walked back into the kitchen, he was more than prepared to do what had to be done. Without a word, he walked towards her with determination. "You assaulted me," he said a split second before he bent down and lifted her up, tossing her over his shoulder.

Dassar could honestly say that he had never been more turned on by a woman in his life. The fact that she was not intimidated by him was the most amazing realization. And it had him fired up to prove that she would obey him.

Luna was too stunned by both his words and his actions to react at first. But when he started for the stairs, panic kicked into overdrive. "What do you think you are doing?" she demanded loudly, pounding him on his back as he carried her through the front room and up the stairs. "Put me down you obnoxious brute!" she practically screamed.

His only response was to smack her on the bottom, which had her head lifting up and her jaw dropping as she felt the sting on her fanny. "You did not just spank me!" she yelped. But as she swung her head up, she realized that they had an audience of guards and Hasif, all of whom were spilling out of the dining room to watch. And every single man was watching with amusement as Dassar carried her up the stairs in an ignominious position. "Oh, you all think this is funny?" she challenged. "Well don't think any of you are getting the gingersnaps I have in the fridge for this afternoon's cookies!"

She had the satisfaction of seeing all of their faces drop in horror a split second before Dassar smacked her bottom once again.

He turned the corner and headed towards his suite and that's when Luna knew she was in a heap of trouble. "Dassar, what do you think you're doing?" she asked, nervousness overriding her anger now. They were heading towards his bedroom now and she wasn't sure what he was planning. "Dassar? Talk to me. I'm sorry about…well, whatever. Just don't…" He did!

He didn't say a word as he opened the door and walked through it. He slammed the door before flopping her down in the middle of the still unmade bed. He didn't wait for her to try and figure out her escape before he followed her down, his arms imprisoning her and his mouth capturing hers.

"No!" she yelled but it was pointless. He wasn't waiting around for her permission and she couldn't stop his powerful shoulders when they leaned down.

His lips captured hers and that was all she was able to say. From that moment on, it was only gasps of pleasure or excitement as he proceeded to kiss every part of her body. Her sweater was gone, tossed away and she had no idea where her plain, white cotton bra went. All she knew was that his mouth was covering her nipple and it was the most intense sensation she'd ever experienced. She arched into his mouth, giving him more of her breast as her eyes closed and her heart rate spiraled out of control.

"Dassar," she whispered, afraid that if she spoke any louder, he might stop the magic he was weaving around her.

"Tell me what you like," he commanded as he pulled her other nipple into his mouth teasing it and rolling it around. His erection was pressed against her core and she pushed against him, wanting something but not really sure what. "Talk to me, Luna. Tell me how to touch you."

"Just there," she gasped and her hands flew up to hold his head in place. "Just like that." And she arched again, but a moment later, it was too much for her and she tried to pull away by wiggling up higher on the bed. He wasn't going to let her do that and his hands grabbed her hips, holding her still and she screamed when his mouth continued to tease her breast, unaware of how loud she was.

"Please don't do that any longer!" she begged him even while her jeans-clad legs were wrapping around his waist, trying to pull him closer. She wasn't aware of his fingers working her jeans off, or of the way her sneakers were tossed far away.

"You are beautiful," Dassar whispered as his hands slid her jeans off of her long, slender legs. His eyes caught on her cotton underwear and he blinked in surprise. "You need to remind yourself of what day it is?" he asked as he read the word "Wednesday" on the plain cotton.

Luna's passion glazed eyes focused slightly and looked up at hm. "Excuse me?" she gasped, trying to understand what he was asking of her. When she realized that his eyes were looking at her hips, and those hips no longer were protected by her jeans, she tried to hide herself with her hands. "You shouldn't be…"

Dassar laughed, throwing back his hands. "You're not allowed to hide yourself from me, Luna," he told her even while his hands pulled hers away, mercilessly leaving her vulnerable to his hungry eyes. "I'm going to see and taste every delectable inch of you."

"You can't do this to me," she whispered, even while her body arched into his mouth when he nibbled on her hipbone.

"You should have let me taste your bread pudding," he teased. "But I have complete faith that you will taste even more delectable."

"Dassar, this is crazy," she gasped, but then his fingers slid along the elastic of her underwear and she froze. Everything inside of her wanted to know what it would feel like if he moved his fingers lower, if he would just… "Yes!" she cried out when his fingers slipped underneath the cotton of her underwear.

"Tell me you want this, Luna," he said, his voice deep and husky.

She was perfectly still while she listened to his words. "I want this, but you can't do it."

Dassar laughed softly. "Those two statements are too contradictory. So I'm going with the first one, Luna." And a moment later, his fingers moved against that part of her that no other man had ever touched. She almost leaped off of the bed as the excitement surged through her and she moved her legs, giving him better access.

42

She wanted him to take her underwear off so that he could do more, she could feel it all, but he didn't move the cotton. His fingers teased and tantalized, but they weren't doing what she needed him to do.

Her hands were gripping the sheets and her hips were shifting, easing his fingers where she needed them the most. But he wouldn't let her have that release. "Are you ever going to deny me again?" he asked, his body aching to bury himself inside of her but he held back, enjoying this almost as much. She was so responsive, just the slightest touch and she was at his mercy, arching into his fingers and practically begging him for more.

"No. Never," she whispered. She had no idea what she was promising. All she knew was that she had to say the right words to get his fingers to move. And when they did, she almost screamed at the new sensation. She was too new at this and couldn't play the games, couldn't slow down her body's reactions. So when his fingers touched that sensitive bud, her body burst apart, her legs clamping down on his hand as her body arched off of the bed, her eyes squeezing shut as she experienced her first orgasm.

When she finally came back to the world, she opened her eyes to find Dassar hovering over her, his hands still touching her and his eyes hot and wild. "That was beautiful," he growled. "I want you to do that again."

Luna shook her head, too shocked by what he'd just done to her. "No, please, don't..." and she tried to pull away from him. Rolling onto her stomach, she was about to crawl away, but then his hand slid enticingly down her spine and all of those crazy sensations rose up once again and she was his prisoner. He didn't need chains or bars, he just needed one finger tracing down the overly sensitive places on her back and she was his.

Dassar lifted her up so that she was kneeling on the bed, her back against his chest so that his hands could roam over her breasts. His teeth nibbled on her neck and shoulders while his hands teased her breasts, her nipples, sliding down her flat stomach until his fingers were once again buried in those secret curls. Luna arched backwards, her hands clenching at his legs as he explored her body once more.

"Tell me you're mine," he growled in her ear.

She shook her head, not really understanding what he was saying when his fingers were exploring her like this. All she knew was that she couldn't think and she wanted that release again but wasn't sure how to tell him what she needed.

"Please don't stop," she begged, hearing the desperation in her voice and not recognizing it as her own.

"Don't worry," he said but he stepped back, tearing off his clothes. "Turn around," he commanded.

Luna did, sitting back on the bed but she was shocked when she saw the dark skin that was now being revealed to her hungry eyes as he peeled of his shirt. When his hands moved to the belt of his slacks, she held her breath and her eyes widened with excitement and more than a little fear.

When he pushed off his slacks and boxers, Luna's eyes widened at all that he revealed. The enormous erection was nothing like anything she'd ever anticipated. Grabbing the sheet, she pulled the material over, trying to cover herself even as she shook her head in denial.

Dassar saw her expression and knew that he'd have to help her through the next step. Moving closer to the bed, he didn't touch her in any way other than to kiss her. He kept kissing her until he felt her tension ease away. And only then did he shift his hands from the mattress to her arms, trailing his fingers down her skin and reigniting the fire that had dimmed when she'd taken in his nakedness.

Pushing her back, he let his hands move down her body, his mouth following. He teased her sensitive breasts, biting and sucking on her nipples until he felt her arch into his mouth again. He almost laughed when her slender legs clamped down on his hand when he tried to tease her down there. But he wasn't giving up. He was in too much pain to stop. He wanted this woman more than he'd ever wanted any other woman in his life. And he was going to have her. But he wanted her to be just as on fire for him too.

"Open up for me, Luna," he coaxed, nipping and sucking, teasing her until she was writhing against him.

His fingers slid inside of her, slowly easing the way for him. One finger, then two, and he stroked her slowly, letting her set the rhythm. When her hips were moving with his fingers, he eased his hand away and replaced it with his erection, watching her carefully. The last thing he wanted right now was to scare her again. He almost roared with need when her legs opened up wider for him, begging him to enter her.

Still he took her slowly, easing in and out, shocked at how tight she was. When he felt the resistance, he looked down at her, noting that her eyes were still closed, her tongue sticking out of her mouth in a way that made him more than a little crazy.

But right now he didn't have the ability to be kind. "Luna, open your eyes!" he commanded, stopping his hips from moving any deeper.

Luna couldn't believe how wonderful this man felt as he filled her up. But he was stopping! Why was he stopping? She opened her eyes and looked at him, unaware of her nails biting into the skin of his biceps that were bulging with the effort to remain perfectly still. She wiggled her hips slightly, needing that friction or something. "You're doing it again," she gasped, moving her hands from his arms to that magnificent chest, her fingers exploring the muscles and ridges there. "You're stopping."

Dassar muttered something in his own language that sounded a bit rude to her but she didn't care. She slid her legs up higher, trying to get him to move again. She liked it when he moved!

"Luna!" he almost roared. "Are you a virgin?" he demanded.

She froze, her startled eyes shifting to his angry face. "Um…" Her hands stilled on the muscles of his sides. "Yes," she whispered. "Is that why you're angry?" she asked, suddenly hurt. "It isn't a problem."

Dassar threw back his head, trying to regain control. This contrary woman was asking if her virginity was a problem? He couldn't believe what was happening to him! He rallied every bit of self-control he had and lowered himself until he could kiss her. "I'm not angry, Luna love," he replied.

"You look angry," she countered. "Get off me," she told him, pushing against his shoulder. But her efforts were completely ineffective. "I don't…"

"I can't, love," he told her and shook his head, trying to clear it of the haze of need. "I can't stop now."

She liked the sound of that. "You can't?" she asked, her blue eyes starting to shine once more. "Good," she whispered. "I don't really want you to stop." She bit her lip, "Unless you want to."

Dassar would have laughed at her adorable expression, if her body wasn't so tight and he wasn't about to roar with the effort to remain absolutely still. "It is going to hurt, love."

She knew this. "Go ahead," she told him, lifting one hand to touch his neck. She was touched that he was so concerned for her. He looked angry, but that wasn't it at all. He was…before she could finish that thought, he pressed into her and broke through the barrier of her body. He absorbed her gasp of pain into his mouth as he kissed her as tenderly as possible, holding still until he felt her body start to relax once again. Lifting his head, his large hands framed her delicate face. "Are you okay?" he asked, knowing that he was almost growling at her but she felt too damn good!

"I'm fine," she said, smiling brightly at him. "Thank you."

Dassar stared down at her, stunned and not sure what to say in reply. She'd just given him the gift of her virginity and…she was thanking him? He should be thanking her, cherishing her and showering her with gifts to show her how he was feeling at the moment. But he couldn't do any of that. Because he was too intent on making love to this woman. Instead of diamonds, he would give her the most amazing climax he possibly could. And as he started moving, slowly at first, he was intent on doing exactly that.

At his first thrust, Luna gasped at the intense pleasure that sparkled through her body. Looking up at him, her mouth open with surprise, she grabbed onto him once more. With every additional thrust, the pleasure only intensified, growing stronger until Luna started shaking her head and pushing him away. "I can't do this, Dassar. You have to stop!"

She lifted her hips with every thrust and sweat broke out on his forehead. "You can, love. Just relax and trust me. I promise," he squeezed his eyes closed, determined to pleasure her. "Just give yourself to me," he coaxed. "Let yourself go."

He pulled her closer and she wrapped her arms around his enormous body. She tried very hard, but the pleasure was too much. But then he thrust into her one more time and she couldn't hold back any longer. Something burst into flames and all of those sparkles that had been blossoming around her just exploded as her body climaxed around him.

Dassar tried to hold back, to give her another orgasm but she just felt too perfect as she throbbed around him. And the sight of her as she arched into his body just pulled him over the edge. There was no holding back after that. In fact, he couldn't believe the intensity of his climax as poured himself into this beautiful, giving woman.

He collapsed on top of her, but aware of how slender and delicate she was, he rolled over so that she was curled up next to him. In those moments as he tried to get his breathing back under control, he realized that, for the first time in his entire adult life, he had forgotten to use protection when making love to a woman.

His arm tightened around her with that thought. It sealed her fate and the tightness in his chest relaxed. There was no more guilt in marrying this woman. She might be too soft, too gentle and filled with unrealistic, romantic hopes. But she might be carrying his child. That eliminated all of his guilt over what he was going to do.

Luna looked up at the ceiling, her breathing ragged and her body still tingling. But her mind was slowing coming back into focus once again. "Dassar, please tell me that we didn't just…"

He almost laughed when she once again tried to pretend something didn't happen. But he still hadn't recovered. His teeth bit into her shoulder gently. "We did," he countered. "Now we have to be married," he said and smoothed his hand down her waist, ending at her bottom before moving back up.

Luna rolled over, staring out the window in an effort to come to the realization of what she'd just done. "We didn't. We'll just pretend like this didn't happen."

He laughed and his hand moved down lower, finding a spot on her waist that tickled. "Just like we didn't kiss yesterday out on the pathway?" he asked, and his nose nudged her arm, making space for his mouth to tease the side of her breast. "And like we didn't kiss yesterday in your kitchen?" His mouth nibbled his way around to the underside of her breast. "Is that how we're pretending?"

She sighed as her head moved backwards, the sensations building again even though she fought them this time. "Dassar, we can't keep doing this."

"Since we will be married by this weekend, we can do this until we are too exhausted to move." And his hand pushed her leg forward, making room for that part of his body that she couldn't ignore.

"Don't!" she gasped even as his finger slid inside of her, finding her wet and ready for him. "Oh please don't stop," she whispered, moving so that his fingers could go deeper into her body.

"Ah, you're going to be quiet this time?" he asked, laughing even while his body slid into her tight, wet heat. "I don't mind. I think I can figure out what your body is telling me even if you're trying to keep quiet."

Luna had no idea what he was saying to her but she didn't care either. His body started moving and her fingers grabbed the sheets, holding on as the waves of intense pleasure threatened to overwhelm her once again. "I don't understand," she said, gritting her teeth as his hands moved up her body. His thumb and forefinger tweaked her nipple and she almost splintered apart with that touch. Her hand reached out, grabbing onto his hand and pressing his fingers flat. But then his fingers spread open, and her fingers pressed his fingers closed, causing her to actually tweak her own nipple and the pleasure sent her right over the edge into mind-blowing pleasure. She was completely unaware of Dassar following behind her with his own climax. All she knew was that he was there, his hands were touching her and he was completely in control of her body. And she loved it!

# Chapter 5

Luna stayed in the kitchen, her fingers flipping through the cookbook laid out on the counter, but her eyes weren't seeing anything. Her mind was too wrapped up in what she'd done all morning and afternoon with Dassar. She couldn't believe what she'd done, all that he'd taught her about herself. She closed her eyes tightly as memories flooded her mind, making parts of her body throb once more with intense need, almost aching!

Unfortunately, her body's betrayal hadn't been the worst part. It wasn't even the fact that, the moment she stepped out of Dassar's room, she wanted to run right back in and beg him to make love to her yet again.

Nor was the fact that she'd ignored all of her morning chores. And her afternoon ones! She still couldn't believe how long they'd spent in bed enjoying each other's bodies. On the bed, in the shower, against the wall trying to get back to the bed, against one of the chairs….Luna blushed painfully as she remembered how many times Dassar had made love to her. So many positions, so many ways….she hadn't even known it was possible to be that crazed and needy.

No, the worst part was when she'd forced her feet to walk down the stairs. She suddenly realized how loud they had been. The inn was old, the walls thin. She'd reinforced them so that not as much noise would come through but the walls weren't sound proofed. She'd discovered that when Melanie, her daytime helper had smiled knowingly when Luna had re-emerged from her private area where she'd showered and changed clothes. "Hi there!" Melanie greeted Luna, pen flipping back and forth in her hand. "How has your day been?" she asked with an enormous grin.

"I need to make beds," Luna said, her voice hoarse because of all the screaming she'd done with Dassar. Goodness, how she'd screamed! She'd yelled, begged, pleaded and screamed with pleasure as his hands moved over her, making her body throb with both pleasure and frustration as he mastered all of the parts of her body. She'd had no idea that there were so many pleasure points on her body!

No matter how long she'd scrubbed her body in the shower earlier, she couldn't get the scent of Dassar off of her skin. But Melanie's smile made her insides clench with embarrassment.

"Someone had a good morning," she said as she stuffed another load of sheets into the dryer.

Luna had frozen with her words then looked up at the ceiling. When she'd remembered how she'd screamed out Dassar's name, she turned a bright pink. "You…heard?"

Melanie laughed but her smile faltered when she saw Luna's expression. "Oh, don't worry about it! No one else was in the inn when I arrived. And even I went to the rooms at the other end of the inn." She brightened. "Don't sweat it. Of all the people in this town, you deserve this the most. You work too hard and you've taken on the responsibility of fixing this mess we've gotten into with the loans. You should take time for yourself."

Luna smiled weakly, not mentioning the strange marriage proposal she'd received from Dassar. She walked out of the laundry room and into her kitchen. Which was why she was sitting there when Dassar finally found her looking through recipes. Or pretending to.

She wasn't really doing anything except trying to figure out how to move her entire business to another town. In another state. And possibly another country. Someplace where no one knew her name and no one would know what she'd done for most of the morning. And afternoon.

Lowering her head into her open palms, she tried taking deep breaths. But it didn't seem to calm her down. "I don't know what to do," she whispered to the empty kitchen.

"Marry me," a deep voice said from the other side of the island.

Luna jerked backwards, staring up at Dassar. Her mouth fell open and she tried to come up with something to say, some words that would dissuade him from such a horrible idea, but she drew a blank. In fact, all her mind could do was contemplate ideas on how to get him back to bed and her cheeks warmed up with that thought.

This wasn't her! She'd thought she was almost anti-sexual since no man had ever stirred anything even closely reminiscent of desire within her. All of the men she'd casually dated over the years had been nice, but she'd left them with a simple kiss, not needing anything more from them because they left her cold.

Not Dassar! And she didn't like who she became when he was around. Or touching her. Or making her scream….

She halted those memories, forcing her mind to remain clean and focused. What had he been asking her? Marriage? Good grief! "No. That's definitely not the solution to the problem," she said firmly and stood up.

"And what is your solution?" he asked.

She took a deep breath and looked down. "Chocolate chip cookies," she said firmly, her hand coming up to smooth over the recipe. "With M&Ms instead of chocolate chips. Or maybe oatmeal raisin." She looked at the pages in question.

"Those are both normal, old-fashioned cookies." And that's what she wanted to be, she thought silently. She wanted to go back to being an old-fashioned woman who didn't have this aching need to pull this man into her arms and do naughty things with him. Things that weren't...normal! She didn't feel normal when he was around her. And she definitely didn't like who she became. It was wrong. It was...indecent!

Dassar spread his arms wide, leaning against the countertop. "Luna, you need to understand one thing very carefully. I am not fooling around with this. If you don't marry me, then I will leave here and the town will fold. I will instruct my bank manager to foreclose on the properties immediately."

Her heart seemed to stop in her chest with his words. She couldn't believe he would do something like that. Not this man. Not the man who had held her in his arms and tenderly taught her about making love. Not the man who had pulled her close, his body intimately connected to hers and urged her to trust him!

"No. You won't do it." She had to believe that. She had to know that the person she'd given her body to earlier today wasn't a mean, horrible man!

Dassar shook his head. "Luna, I have an entire country to build back up. Don't romanticize me. Don't make me into a hero. That's not who I am," he told her softly, but with a tone of voice that demonstrated the truth of is words. "I have to marry. And I have to produce an heir. You are the one I've chosen and it is imperative that I make this happen quickly. It won't be a love match because I don't do love. I have worked hard to make my country work better, to create jobs and opportunities. I don't have time for love or softness. But I will treat you right and this town will thrive once they are no longer under the burden of their heavy debts."

He didn't like the tears that formed in her beautiful, cat-like eyes with his words but he wouldn't take them back. "Come here," he said gently. He wouldn't take no for an answer, even when she stepped back, out of his reach. He took another step and gently but firmly took her hand in his, pulling her closer. "Hey," he said as he wrapped his strong arms around her. "It is going to be okay."

She shuddered and gave in to his comforting embrace. "No. It isn't going to be okay. From what you're saying now, I'm caught in this horrible limbo where I either marry a stranger or let the town I love go down in flames."

He laughed at her version of her options. "It isn't as bad as all that, is it?" he asked, running his hands through her unusual hair, amazed at how she was soft and silky everywhere. Except her hands, he remembered. Those hands were red and chapped from hard work and he didn't like that at all. He wanted her hands to be just as soft as the rest of her and he would do anything it took to heal those hands of hers.

Luna buried her face in his chest, breathing in the clean scent of this man. "Yes," she sniffed. "It is horrible." She couldn't stop the tears now that they'd started. "You're horrible and I can't believe that you've cornered me like this." She rubbed her nose and tears against his pristine shirt, uncaring what she might have done to him. And she couldn't believe that she was finding comfort in the arms of the very same man creating her terror. "Please don't do this to me," she begged him.

His hand slid up and down her back, coming to rest against her bottom. "I have to. It is imperative that we preserve the peace among the four countries affected by the war. My marriage and a son will help to do that."

She squeezed her eyes closed. "And I'm your tool for doing that." She hated this man at this moment. He didn't answer her. There was no need.

# Chapter 6

Dassar found her later that afternoon out in the chicken yard, throwing chicken feed across the muddy area. "I have to return to Altair," he explained, his lips compressing as she tossed yet another handful of chicken feed out to the birds.

Luna's hand froze. She'd thought that she couldn't be hurt any more by this man, but she was shocked at how deep the pain went with that announcement.

But this would be a good thing, she told herself, suppressing the pain and sadness that threatened to overwhelm her.

What a ridiculous reaction, she told herself firmly. She wasn't sad! She was perfectly fine! In fact, the faster he left, the more quickly she could get her life back in order.

"When?" she asked, trying to figure out how much time she had to come up with another solution. She tossed another handful of feed, then wiped her hands on her apron and locked up the bin.

Maybe he would go back to Altair or whatever his country was for a little while and she could find another bank, someone else who would loan her and the rest of the town the money. They didn't need much. Maybe if she just asked for a loan small enough to cover six months' worth of payments. That might get everyone back up on their feet. Or maybe she could borrow a bit more and start an advertising campaign.

Dassar stepped back and looked down at the woman. "We leave tomorrow night," he told her and walked towards the door to the inn again. At the doorway, he turned back for a moment. "It will be okay, Luna. I'll make it so." He pulled back and looked down at her. "I have some work to do and calls to make but I'll take you out to dinner tonight and we'll discuss the details." And then he was gone.

She brightened with those words. Tomorrow night, right after he left, she could get the townspeople together and they could brainstorm on where to go next. By the time he returned, she could have all of the funding in place and she could tell him he'd have to find another woman to marry.

She almost doubled over as the pain stabbed at her. She hated pushing Dassar away, not wanting him to even touch another woman as he'd touched her earlier.

She was stunned by the intensity of her anger, but squeezed her eyes shut, knowing that he would have to eventually marry someone else.

Okay, so the idea of another woman in his arms, doing the things with him that he'd done with her earlier today actually made her sick to her stomach but she had to do this! She couldn't marry a man who…didn't love her?

Goodness, what was she thinking? She didn't love him either. Luna's cheeks turned pink as she remembered their morning, and afternoon, together. That wasn't love, she told herself. That was simple lust.

Okay, so she cared about him. And she cared about his opinion of her. She wouldn't have been so hurt about the other pastries if she didn't care. It suddenly occurred to her that he still hadn't tasted her maple syrup bread pudding. She knew she'd baked it especially for him this morning. Luna had wanted to impress him. But by the time she'd come back downstairs after being with Dassar for hours, and she sighed as those memories hit her full force once more, the bread pudding, along with everything else she'd baked this morning, was gone. Not even a scone to be had.

Luna turned to her fridge. She had to work this out. She had just a few hours until he left and she wasn't going to be caught unaware again.

Around five o'clock, she had just finished cleaning the kitchen after prepping tomorrow's breakfast. Her kitchen was clean, Melanie was taking care of the front desk and all of the animals were fed. There really wasn't anything more she could do. She had no other excuses but to get ready for dinner with Dassar tonight.

Making her way to her private area, she showered once again and changed into a pretty, red dress that clung to her curves. She dried her hair and fluffed it around her shoulders. Adding a touch of mascara, lipstick and, after looking at her face carefully, dabbed on some concealer and powder since her eyes were a bit more tired looking than she'd like.

As she stared at herself in the mirror, she considered changing her dress. Was it too revealing? Was she sending a message that she might not want to send? The material was clingy and molded to her breasts and waist before flaring out. She tugged the red fabric over her breasts a bit more, not wanting her cleavage to show quite so much.

"Don't do that," Dassar's deep voice spoke from the doorway.

Luna swung around, startled to see him in her bedroom. Goodness, she was stunned once again by his height and how broad his shoulders were. She now knew that those shoulders and arms were covered with muscles and that stomach was flat except for the ridges of muscles that indented his abdomen. He was an extremely fine specimen of manhood and she shivered with memories once again.

Her mind, stunned by his sudden presence, went into furious overdrive at his arrogance in entering her private area without permission. "You're not supposed to be back here," she whispered, wishing that her voice was stronger. And she really wished that her body didn't tighten with anticipation just at the sight of him. She tried to hold onto her anger, but everything inside of her was fully aware of him as a man, as the man who had shown her a side of her she hadn't thought possible.

Dassar ignored her comment and moved into the bedroom, stopping when he was standing in front of her. She moved backwards, but her dresser stopped any sort of real retreat.

"You're late," he replied, his dark eyes heated and roaming over her figure in the red dress. "But I can appreciate why. You look beautiful." His hand lifted, touching her soft, almost-white hair. "I thoroughly approve."

She meant to pull away from him, to pull her hair out of his fingers but she found herself leaning into his caress instead. "I was going to change my dress."

His eyes dropped back down to her breasts and she instantly regretted her comment because those eyes made her nipples harden and the peaks were now showing through the thin material.

"I don't see any reason to change. But if you'd like to take the dress off, I have no objections." His hands moved to the tie at her waist but her smaller hands quickly grabbed his wrists.

"We can't," she whispered.

One black eyebrow rose with her words. "Can't?" he asked softly, his fingers still fiddling with the tie.

"Shouldn't," she finally revised. She was quickly learning that this man was up for any challenge. Telling him he couldn't do something only made him need to prove that he could. And would!

The half-smile that formed on those masculine lips made her body ache even more. "That's all a matter of opinion."

Her hands tightened on his, not sure what to say to him. "I thought we were going to dinner," she latched onto that excuse, needing to get him out of her bedroom. Because right now, the bed behind him was looking extremely enticing! She had to remove herself from that temptation because her body was already swaying closer to him, wanting to feel that extraordinary pleasure once again. He'd done things to her body this morning that she wanted to experience again, stunned that she'd been missing out on those feelings all her life.

"We are. But perhaps we should…"

Luna knew exactly where he was going with that comment and she stopped him. "I haven't eaten all day long. I'm very hungry."

His hands instantly froze and his eyes widened slightly. "Nothing at all?" he demanded.

Luna suddenly realized that he was actually angry with her. For not eating? Good grief, it was his fault, she thought as he stepped back and took her hand. He's

54

the one who had kept her in bed during breakfast and then she'd been too upset to eat anything for lunch. And to be honest, she wasn't terribly hungry for food now. She pretty much lost her appetite for anything but him when he was around, which didn't bode well for her plan to stay out of his arms.

"Well..." she started to say something but he stopped her with what she suspected was a curse although she didn't understand it because it wasn't in English.

"We will dine immediately," he commanded, leading her out of the bedroom. She only had time to grab her wrap and her purse before he was dragging her out of the inn and handing her into a long, beautiful limousine.

Inside, he opened a compartment and took out a bottle of orange juice, pouring it into a crystal glass for her. "Drink this," he told her as he handed it to her. "You cannot go without food, Luna. This isn't healthy."

She took the glass and sipped the liquid, grateful for the cool juice. "You're right," she said, not sure if she was relieved at his hasty exit or disappointed. But she sat there in silence as the darkness surrounded the two of them.

"What did you do today?" she asked, not liking the way he was glaring at her in the darkness.

"I spoke with the prime minister of Great Britain about oil sales and bought property in France for a new refinery."

She swallowed the orange juice, shocked at his words. "Oh." She thought about that for a moment, so surprised that she was stunned for a long moment. "Kind of trumps the new recipe I found," she said softly, feeling completely inadequate all of a sudden.

He could feel her sadness and he didn't like it. Not one little bit! And he was even more annoyed that he cared. He'd never observed a woman before, unconcerned if they were feeling anything outside of the bedroom. He'd never had the time. During the war, all of his energy was focused on protecting his people and his country. Women were a necessary distraction, but he'd given them as little of his time as possible. And after the war, every moment of his days and most of his nights were taken up in efforts to repair his country, bring back a healthy economy and ensure that his people were safe, getting educated and had enough food to eat. Again, women were to alleviate his sexual frustration so he could concentrate on his responsibilities. Nothing more, nothing less. He ensured that they enjoyed the experience but he moved on, barely thinking about them unless he needed them.

That was why Faris had been such a perfect mistress, he realized. She didn't pull any of his energy towards concern. He could focus everything on his people, on getting them back to a peace they deserved.

So why was the idea of going back to Faris so abhorrent? Why was this little woman with her shaking hands and her soft, blue eyes getting to him?

With a muttered curse, he lifted her up, settling her onto his lap once again. He barely took the time to take the glass of juice out of her hands, setting it aside before he focused all of his attention on Luna. Kissing this woman just seemed like the only reasonable response to her worries. He simply couldn't stand to see her nervous or anxious in any way.

Luna almost dropped the glass of juice when he picked her up but he carefully set the glass aside before his mouth covered hers. She moaned at the first touch of his lips against hers, still surprised at how amazing it felt to be in his arms.

Unconsciously, she turned, curling into his arms and kissed him back with all of the confusion and need and desire that had been plaguing her during the afternoon. All of the questions she couldn't answer, all of the strange sensations, were thankfully obliterated when he kissed her. She didn't want the kiss to stop because as soon as it did, those questions and confusion, her humiliation at needing him so much in such a short time would resurface and she'd be back to where she was.

So when he started to lift his mouth, she reached up and touched his jaw, silently pleading with him not to stop. And he didn't. The kiss went on and on. The sensations throughout her body were shocking to her but when she felt his fingers on her waist, she shifted so that he could touch her more. And when his hand moved higher, covering her breast, she whimpered with need, with the clawing ache that shifted to be centered between her legs. Luna couldn't believe how much she needed his touch, his kiss and she moved against him, wanting so much more than just these not-so-innocent touches.

Dassar couldn't hold back, not when she was moving against him, her body and those sounds in the back of her throat telling him that she wanted this. He'd meant for tonight to be only conversation. He needed her to realize that they were leaving tomorrow and she would be his wife. But his hand slipped underneath that incredible red fabric, his fingers unerringly searching for and finding her nipple and he couldn't stop testing that amazing skin, loving the way it puckered under his touch and her body shifted so that he had better access, so that her breast pressed against his hand, silently inviting him for more.

The limousine stopped and he lifted his head, looking around. He muttered a curse before lifting her up. She was so dazed that he had the honor of adjusting her dress to cover those amazing breasts only moments before his guards opened the door for him.

He practically lifted her out of the seat and steadied her when she had trouble standing. He realized that even her eyes were a bit unfocused and pride that he'd done this to her swamped him.

Damn, he liked that about her! She wasn't able to hide her reactions to his touch and it turned him on more than any woman ever had in the past. Tucking her hand onto his arm, he led her into the restaurant. He wanted to feed her and then get her back so he could make love to her again. Which was odd, since he'd told himself that he wasn't going to make love to her again until they were wed tomorrow but he hadn't anticipated kissing her in the limousine either.

Luna entered the normally busy restaurant and looked around. It was small, but whenever she'd come here in the past, there had been an hour or more wait for a table. There was no one here!

"Where is everyone?" she asked, noting that the waiters and chefs were even hidden. The host bowed when they walked inside, but he was the only person she could see.

"This way, Your Highness," the host said and led them to a table by the crackling fireplace.

Dassar held her chair out for her and pushed it in as she sat down before moving to the other chair. "We requested that all the tables be reserved for the night," he explained.

Her mouth dropped open. "Dassar, it is Wednesday night! It isn't even this slow on Monday or Tuesday night!"

He snapped his linen napkin open. "The owner was well compensated." He accepted the menu from the waiter who also had an open bottle of wine. He poured some into both of their glasses before walking away, giving them privacy.

She couldn't believe that this man had bought out all of the tables at the most expensive restaurant in the area, just so he could dine with her. It just didn't make sense. "Why did you do this?" she asked.

Dassar was reviewing the menu items but he said, "I didn't do this. I believe my security guards were wary of the crowds in this restaurant and concerned about how to protect the two of us. They arranged this. But I don't mind," he said, looking up after having made his selection to look at her across the table. "It allows me to talk to you without interruptions or worry that anyone will overhear our conversation. This topic isn't one that anyone else needs to hear."

She swallowed painfully, a lump in her throat inhibiting more motion. "I don't think I'm ready to discuss that topic," she said and took a long swallow of her wine.

He leaned back and watched her, thinking that he wasn't going to allow her to get drunk and avoid tonight's conversation. "We must discuss it, Luna," he told her firmly. "Our wedding is tomorrow. We can't avoid it any longer."

Her hands started shaking and she set the wine glass down on the table. "I thought you were leaving tomorrow." That's what he'd said! He couldn't go back on his word!

"I am leaving tomorrow. With you as my wife." He let those words float around the table, watching her reactions carefully. It wasn't as if he had to guess at her thoughts. She was so gentle and kind, and all of her expressions told him exactly what she was thinking. Luna was beautiful, but she was also too soft. He would have to toughen her up so she would survive. And tonight was her first lesson.

Her hands were shaking in reaction so she hid them under the table, not wanting him to see how terrified she was at the topic. "I thought I would have more time to think about this."

His eyes were hard as he shook his head, denying her need for more time. "You've thought about it. There are only two options." He saw the way her pretty white teeth nibbled on her lower lip and he almost laughed out loud at how obvious she was. "No other bank will offer you a bridge loan, Luna." Her eyes snapped up to his and he knew that his guess was perfectly on target. "Is that what you were hoping?"

She slumped down in her chair. "You're not giving me much of a choice."

He couldn't relent, wouldn't let himself be affected by her desperate gaze. This was too important for his people, he told himself. "Everyone has choices." Her answer wasn't important to him, he reminded himself. He wasn't emotionally involved. He would not allow himself to fall in…to become emotionally involved in any way. He wouldn't even use that word.

Luna's blue eyes glared at him, all her confusion and worry coalescing into red-hot fury at the pompous way he was manipulating this conversation. And her life! "Oh right! The choice to marry a stranger and move my life to a foreign country and uncertain future or to let my friends lose their dreams and their livelihoods. What about my dreams?" she demanded.

The waiter started to approach the table so she snapped her mouth closed. "I don't want anything to eat," she told him, leaning back and crossing her arms over her chest. "Why don't you just take me home? You don't need to keep up the pretense of being a nice guy. I see your true colors now."

He purposely kept his face blank, ignoring the sharp stab of guilt he felt in the vicinity of his stomach, or perhaps his heart, at her words. She was trembling and he knew he could solve all of her problems with a simple word. But he wanted her. He wanted her as his wife. Quite desperately. And he needed this to happen. Two of the others were already wed with heirs on the way and he suspected the fourth would be wed very soon. He couldn't wait any longer. He had to fulfill the terms of the treaty and reassure his people. If that meant being merciless, well, he'd done worse things in his life.

But he could soften the choice for her.

"What are you going to have for dinner?"

"I'm not hungry," she repeated, trying not to pout but she was feeling trapped and she didn't like it.

He waved the waiter to the table. "We'll both have the steak," he told the man who nodded quickly and backed away. Turning back to Luna, he watched her carefully. "What are your dreams, little one?"

She stiffened with his endearment. "I'm not 'little'!" she snapped, "and I doubt you're truly interested in my dreams. Otherwise, we wouldn't be having this conversation."

He paused, wanting to give her the world but knowing that his people had to take priority. "I can make it better," he promised, but he kept his voice hard, uncompromising. She had to accept that this marriage was going to happen. Even now, his body hardened with the idea that she might be pregnant with his child. The thought of her slender body growing large with his child was the most erotic thing he'd ever considered. She would be beautiful during pregnancy, he suspected. And she would be an excellent mother. The way she took care of the animals and the entire town proved to him that her heart was filled with the need to care and to love.

She kept her eyes down on the table, unable to look at him. "You are willing to walk away and drop all the debts we owe?" she asked, already knowing the answer.

"No. But I'm willing to make you happy."

Her eyes snapped up to his. "How?"

He took her hand, not letting it go when she tried to tug it away. "You will be royalty, Luna, with all of the benefits that go along with that station in the world."

She snorted. "Girls dream of being princesses but that's not my dream, Dassar."

"What are your dreams?" he asked gently.

Luna sighed and was about to speak when their steaks arrived more quickly than she'd thought possible. It looked perfect with some elaborate potatoes on the side and beautifully steamed asparagus. Normally, a meal like this would be exciting and she would be savoring every bite. Unfortunately, she was too upset to eat. The idea actually made her stomach churn.

"My dreams are to live in my small town, get married to a great guy and have children, raise them up to be decent kids who contribute to the world in a positive way." He was about to say something when she interrupted him with another dream. "And to bake whatever strikes my fancy without ever having to clean another toilet in my life."

He chuckled at that last part as he released her hand. "I can give all of that to you except for the small town, although I would wager that the palace might seem like a small town with all of the people that live and work there."

Her interest was caught despite her anger. "You really live in a palace?" she asked, picking up her fork and moving the asparagus away from her potatoes. They might look pretty, but she hated asparagus. In fact, she wasn't a big fan of many vegetables.

"Yes. And work there. My security detail doesn't like it when I venture outside, but I do it whenever possible."

"Why?"

"Because I want to see firsthand what is going on with my people. I want to know that they are being taken care of and thriving. And I can't do that from reports written by someone else. I want to see it all and know personally what is happening in my country."

She had to admit that his attitude was really...awesome. "That's very admirable," she said, cutting into her steak. She could honestly say she'd never seen a steak cooked so perfectly before and she cut a small bite, just to taste it. "Can you tell me what it's like in the palace?" she asked, trying to find something that might make her feel better about this whole situation.

Dassar was relieved when she started eating and wondered about his concern. In the end, the tension in his shoulders relaxed when she took her second bite of the beef relaxed and he attributed that only to the fact that she needed food to keep herself healthy if she really were pregnant. Nothing more, nothing less, he promised himself.

Answering her question, he tried to think of aspects of her future life that would make her feel more comfortable. "We'll have our own suite of rooms that is at the far end of the palace so that most of the staff won't bother us," he explained. And he proceeded to tell her the history of the palace, how it was built, all the funny and horrible things that had happened in that building. He enjoyed the way her features softened as she listened to his stories so he continued, thinking back to all of the history lessons he'd had as a child.

Luna had to admit that she truly loved the history part of it all. It sounded very romantic in a sometimes brutal way but since those days were far behind, she could smile over them now. And the funny things he told her helped her remember that all of the people that worked and resided inside the palace were just humans. They had no special powers that she should be nervous about. Just regular people trying to govern a country as best as possible.

"And you like living there?" she asked.

The question startled him because it had never occurred to him to live anywhere other than the palace. It had never been an option. "I travel all over the world a great deal, but the palace is my home."

That was an intriguing statement. "How often to you get to travel?" Oh, what she wouldn't give to travel more! She'd never been outside of Virginia except to drive to the beaches in North Carolina. Well, and her trek from New York but she didn't want to remember that horrible period in her life. And she didn't think that counted as travel either. Not really.

He recognized the excitement in her eyes, the way her whole body seemed to come alive at the mention of traveling. "Yes. That's another advantage. You will be traveling with me, if you'd like. You'd meet the leaders of other countries, see anything you'd like and you'd have an unlimited wardrobe. As my wife, I want you dressed perfectly at all times."

She sighed and put her knife and fork down, depressed with his words. "That's something about me you might not like, Dassar," she said. "I don't like dressing up. I prefer jeans and a tee-shirt or sweatshirt."

"And while you are in the kitchens baking whatever you like for the palace staff, you can wear tee-shirts and sweatshirts, jeans, whatever you are comfortable in. But when we are in front of the world, you will be representing Altair. You need to show the world that we are a modern, powerful country so your presence, your appearance will need to reflect that prosperity."

She nodded her head, thinking that wasn't asking too much of a person. "So, what you're saying is that I can dress any way I want but when I go out into the world, I need to wear beautiful clothes and look pretty?"

He chuckled at her interpretation. "That pretty much sums it up. Would that be too difficult for you?"

She sighed. "I'm not good at shopping."

He waved that argument aside. "I never shop. My clothes appear in my closet. I imagine that my personal assistant arranges for new clothes to arrive. You will have a personal assistant as well as a whole staff to help you. Including nannies to help with raising our children."

Her eyes flashed with that. "Nannies are not going to raise our children!" she said with a heat she hadn't felt in a long time. "Children are gifts and should not be shuffled off for convenience!"

He smiled, relieved that she felt that way. It made her even more attractive in his eyes. "I agree," he replied softly. "But you also need to be realistic. There will be many times when your presence is needed by my side. A nanny, someone who is trained to handle and raise children in our situation, will be invaluable and will put your mind at ease when you need to be gone."

Her eyes widened. "How often will that happen?" she asked, fearful that her children would be raised by strangers. "And how are we to impress upon our children our own values if someone else is raising them?"

Dassar was relieved to hear her consistently use the terms "our" and "us" when referring to their children. It seemed as if she'd turned a corner, accepting his proposal. He knew that he hadn't given her much of a choice, but it was still a relief to hear. He suddenly realized that he cared if she accepted.

"How was your steak?" he asked.

Luna looked down, surprised to find that she'd eaten the entire steak as well as all of the potatoes. "Um…it was pretty good," she told him but she couldn't remember eating any of it.

"I take it you don't like asparagus?" he teased.

Luna squinched up her nose. "Not even a little. That might be a pretty severe point against me. I don't eat vegetables. I can't. I hate them and I won't do it."

He laughed. "Luna, you don't seem to grasp the whole royalty concept as fully as you should. When we go somewhere," he explained, "your preferences will be conveyed by your assistant. So not only will you never have to eat anything you don't like, it won't even be on your plate. All preferences will be catered to when you are with me."

"You have a whole bunch of bodyguards. And you mentioned palace security."

"Yes," he replied, not sure where she was going with that statement.

"Does that mean that others are trying to hurt you?" She knew the correct word was "kill" but she simply couldn't use that term in reference to a living, breathing person sitting in front of her. It was too horrifying.

Dassar was careful now, not wanting to frighten her in any way, but he had to be honest with her as well. "Yes. I have many enemies and there are still people who are trying to topple our government. We don't always know who they are, but they are out there and they are more than willing to hurt me if they can." He wasn't going to sugar coat that part of their lives. It is an inescapable aspect of his life – and hers from this moment forward. "But it isn't something I worry about. I rely on my guards to keep me safe. Which is why we are here in this restaurant alone instead of surrounded by people who my guards couldn't run background checks on."

Her eyes lifted to his. "Did your guards do a background check on me?"

"Yes," he replied without hesitation. "Anyone who comes into contact with you or me from this point forward, and our children when they are born, will be thoroughly investigated."

She shivered, thinking about what a horrible invasion of privacy that was. "What did your security team find out about me?" she asked, worried that they knew all of her secrets.

"I don't know. Your name would never have been brought up to me as a potential wife if there was anything in your background that was unacceptable." He watched with fascination as the pink coloring stole up her cheeks. He laughed softly. "Luna, is there something in your past that you're embarrassed about?"

She shook her head. "No! Of course not," she told him. "I just…when I was in high school, I wasn't the best student around." There was no way she would tell this man about her father, the way he used to smack her around after her mother left. That was a part of her life that was over and done with.

He waited a moment, hoping she would continue but he had to prompt her. "I didn't read the report, so why don't you tell me what happened in high school. Obviously, the boys didn't realize what a treasure you were."

She turned a darker shade of pink and lowered her lashes. "No. I wasn't a horrible student. I was shy and self-conscious. The boys didn't really notice me all that much. That's one of the reasons I like running the inn. It gives me a chance to talk with the guests, to make them feel comfortable. In high school, and to a lesser extent in college, I was the girl who stood on the sidelines of dances, if I even attended. I had my friends, but none of us were the popular girls. We were the awkward ones. We were the ones that had more fun playing Monopoly on the weekends than playing drinking games with the boys."

"I'm very appreciative of those Monopoly games," he told her and picked up her hand again, lacing his fingers through hers. "If you had played the games with the other boys, you wouldn't be all mine."

She frowned at his comment. "About that," she started to say but the waiter arrived, clearing their dinner plates. He also handed each of them a list of the desserts and Luna started to shake her head. She loved sweets but she didn't think it was a very feminine quality. She always turned down desserts with her dates, pretending to not eat sugar.

"We'll have one of everything on your menu," he told the waiter, not even bothering to look at the options.

The man was confused and stood there for a long moment, staring at Dassar. But then he blew out some air and bowed a bit. "Yes, sir. I mean, Your Highness," and he immediately started backing away. "Right away."

Luna was so stunned at the idea of having all of those desserts brought to their table that she could barely say anything.

He winked at her as he gently squeezed her fingers. "I could see the hope in your eyes, Luna." He chuckled when her shoulders sagged slightly. "Admit it, you have a horrible sweet tooth, don't you?" And he thought it was endearing. She was so slender and lovely, found pleasure in making decadent foods for others, but he suspected that she denied herself the pleasure of tasting each of them more often than not.

She looked down, wondering what else he could see there. She was too open, she thought. A man like him would take advantage of that openness. And then the truth of her future hit her. He was forcing her to marry him! He'd spent a great deal of the morning making love…or more specifically, having sex with her. What other "taking advantage" could he do? He'd pretty much topped all of the high points of a person's life.

"What are you thinking about now, Luna" he asked.

Luna shook her head. If he didn't know, she definitely wasn't going to tell him. A woman needed a few secrets, she thought resentfully. "Okay, so why does the wedding have to be tomorrow?"

"I told you, I have to fly back to Altair tomorrow evening."

She nodded her head and blinked rapidly to stop the tears from flowing. She'd always pictured her wedding to be a fun afternoon or evening where the whole town turned out and she was wearing a floating wedding dress, her hair was pulled up on top of her head with flowers instead of a veil. And most importantly, she was smiling and excited about the event.

Tomorrow would be a very practical affair, she suspected. A judge in some cold, anonymous office with his security guards as witnesses instead of friends and family. It would probably be better this way, she told herself. If the people in the town knew what was really happening, they might ask questions. They would be worried for her and might do something that would jeopardize the very futures on which she was trying to ensure. "Fine," she told him.

Dassar wanted her to talk to him, to tell him what he could do to make tomorrow better for her but he suspected that the only way that was going to happen was if he released her from the wedding.

Thankfully, the desserts arrived at that moment and her eyes lit up with excitement at all of the creative, beautiful desserts. There were pink cupcakes with frosting on top that looked impressively like a real rose, a chocolate mousse with a chocolate "wave" on top, a tiny cake with strawberries cut to look like butterflies, and perfect little white chocolate pyramids with edible gold leaf on the top for decoration.

"Oh my," she sighed. "Everything looks too amazing to actually eat."

Dassar leaned back in his chair and watched her with amusement. "Please tell me that you're not going to leave any of that untouched. It would be a crime," he told her.

She laughed, the first time all night, but she picked up her fork and took a bite of the strawberry cake. "Goodness, this is delicious," she sighed. She opened her eyes and cut another bite, carefully placing it on her fork. "Aren't you going to have any?" she asked, lifting the cake to her mouth.

But that bite never reached her mouth. Dassar grabbed her wrist and pulled the fork over to his mouth. Luna watched with shock as his mouth closed over the strawberry cake, his eyes holding hers captive the whole time.

"Oh," she sighed, her body ramped back up to that intense tingling sensation once more.

He chuckled as he replied, "Oh." When she hesitated to eat more, he took matters into his own hands. He took his own fork and cut a piece of the cupcake for her.  Lifting it to her mouth, he watched with fascination as her lips closed over the fork, taking the sweet into her mouth.

"Why?" she whispered, trying to understand how he could do this to her so completely every time he touched her.

Unfortunately, Dassar's answer didn't help at all.  His simple, "I don't know," were not the words she wanted to hear.

# Chapter 7

Luna woke up at her normal time and stared at the beautiful white dress in the darkness.  She couldn't believe that this was her wedding day.  And she'd only met her groom a few days ago.  It was so surreal, she couldn't quite wrap her mind around it.

Of all the different ways she'd pictured her wedding day, this cold, unromantic proposal, this horrible, demeaning process would not have even entered her mind.  How had her world changed so dramatically in just two days?  She'd been feeding the chickens!  She'd been baking and humming that morning.  She'd made the beds and cleaned the bathrooms…she'd done everything right!

So how could everything be so wrong now?  Looking around her room, she couldn't stop the tears as she thought about her future.  Dassar was not the man she'd thought him to be when she'd first seen him.

Or maybe he was!  Maybe the hardness, the ruthless man was there and she'd just been too silly and wrapped up in her romantic fantasies to see the real person.

Well, she was marrying the real man.  All of the benefits of her future couldn't seem to ease the sadness she felt at the prospect of a marriage without love.

She sighed and stared up at the ceiling, ignoring the beautiful dress that had been waiting for her when she'd come back from dinner last night with Dassar.  He hadn't made love to her last night.  He'd left her at her door with a gentle kiss and a promise that he would make it as right as he could.

What did that even mean?  How could he make things right?  How could he change this reality so that it was palatable to her?  It was impossible!  He was just a ruthless man who needed a bride and she was the most vulnerable!  She'd been the stupid one who had contacted him, raised herself to his awareness and so she had to face the future because she'd done this to herself!  She'd put herself into this position by contacting him in the first place.

So instead of dwelling on the issue and letting her mind start to panic, she slid out of bed and jumped into the shower.  She would make breakfast and get things ready, pretend that it was just an ordinary day.  If she started to think otherwise, she would start to cry and she simply couldn't do that.  Not today.  And probably not for a long time. She needed to learn to be tough, strong. And she needed to stop showing her emotions and thoughts on her face. Dassar could read her too easily! She'd put herself into a vulnerable position with her mortgage and now she was hurting. She absolutely would not be vulnerable to him again!

When she was dressed in leggings and an oversized sweatshirt, she moved into the kitchen and pulled the sausage and egg casseroles out of the fridge, sliding them into the oven. She hadn't even pre-heated the oven as she normally would but she didn't care. She was baking and cooking. That was her job this morning. Tomorrow would bring something else, she had no idea what. But today, it was just routine. She needed this routine, this everyday task that comforted her.

"What are you doing?" Dassar demanded when he walked into the kitchen a few minutes later.

She glanced up at him, then back down at the cheesy potato casserole she was preparing. She hadn't meant to make this, but it just occurred to her and it kept her hands busy. "I'm making breakfast," she told him as if that were the most obvious thing in the world.

"You do not need to make breakfast on our wedding day, Luna," he told her, looking at her red, chapped hands, clenching his jaw so that he wouldn't say anything that might hurt her feelings.

Luna looked up and noticed that he had several papers in his hands. "What are you doing?" she asked defensively. He was working, she thought! He was going through contracts or business documents, all the while, admonishing her for being in the kitchen and doing something she loved.

Dassar didn't even bother to look down. "That isn't the point," he came right back.

"That's exactly the point," she argued. "I have a house full of people who are going to be hungry in a few minutes. So I'm making breakfast."

"Luna, this isn't your job any longer."

She snapped and spun around to argue with him, her anger at how he'd manipulated her world coming out in her fury. "It is my job until one o'clock this afternoon!" she stated forcefully. "I know that you need a wife and I know that you've pulled things together and there's a crazy expensive white dress hanging in my room that I didn't choose and I have no idea how it got there. But right now, at this moment in time, I am the owner of this inn," she told him, ignoring the way her voice broke at the words. She took a deep breath, gathering up her resolve like a protective barrier. "And I'm going to make breakfast for those men out there and if there are any leftovers, I'm going to take them to a friend's house and then I'm going to…" she couldn't think of what she would do next and it wouldn't matter because her inability to ignore today's events broke through her control and she started crying.

Dassar saw the way her eyes glistened and her chin wobbled but she turned away before he could see anything more. But he knew that she was crying and, against his better judgment, he tossed his papers onto the island, walking over to her and wrapped his arms around her as he pulled her close.

"It's going to be okay," he promised. And as her slender body shook with the sobs she couldn't contain any longer, he swore to himself that he would make it okay for her. Somehow, he would make it up to her.

When the crying finally subsided, he pulled back and watched as she wiped her tears on her sweatshirt sleeve. He was fascinated with the way she pulled herself together once more. Women had cried buckets of tears over the years, all of them trying to manipulate him in some way to suit their own purpose. But as Dassar watched this tiny woman with the bright, shining eyes pat her cheeks dry, he knew he'd never been as affected as he was at this moment. He wanted to comfort her and make things right but "right" was only a relative term.

"Okay, that's over with," she told him and took a deep breath. "I need to get things moving or your men are going to be hungry."

"Luna, you don't need to make breakfast for my men. And in a few hours, they will be working for you. They can get breakfast somewhere else."

Luna had already turned back to the stove but she stopped as if she were waiting for something. He wasn't sure what.

When she turned back to him, she looked like he'd just slapped her and his gut twisted painfully. "I know that your men can get food anywhere else. But right now, they are under my roof. And I derive a great deal of pleasure in feeding people and seeing the look of joy on their faces when they try my scrumptious foods. So if you don't mind, I would really like to just go through my normal routine this morning." She took a deep breath as if she were trying to calm herself down. "I will be dressed and ready by one o'clock this afternoon. From that moment on, I will do my best to be your wife and represent your people," she looked back at him, "as long as you agree to wipe out the debt of every shop owner and homeowner in this town."

His eyes shuttered with those words. He wasn't sure why, but he was hoping she would be a bit happier about becoming his wife and want to enter into that role for reasons other than to save her precious town. But that wasn't the deal, he reminded himself. "That was the agreement," he told her.

She nodded her head, ignoring the stab of pain at the almost sad expression in his eyes. She didn't understand why he would be sad or even care about this wedding. They were getting married to seal the deal on some stupid peace treaty for a country she didn't care about and had never even considered visiting. This was her life now though so she would suck it up and carry on.

Straightening her shoulders, she grabbed the hot-pads and reached into the oven to adjust one of the oven shelves to make more room for the potato casserole. It would take at least an hour to cook and she wanted the entire dining room to smell good by the time the men walked in to eat.

Eight hours after she'd stepped out of bed, Luna was dressed in the most beautiful dress she'd ever seen. Dassar had even arranged for a woman to come and do her hair. The woman tried to do Luna's makeup, but she put her foot down, telling the woman that she didn't wear a lot to begin with so she could do that all by herself. It was her last act of rebellion against Dassar's machinations and she felt good for standing up for herself.

When she stepped out of her bedroom, she fought the tears, forcing a smile to her face. Tears were pointless, she told herself. They didn't do any good so there was no reason to waste energy on them.

It was time she got herself under control. Time to get married, she told herself. When she walked through the inn to the front door, she was startled to find two of the men still waiting for her. "Shouldn't you be with Dassar?" she asked.

The men bowed slightly. "We are your guards, my lady," the taller man explained.

That was news to her, she thought. She had guards! Who would have thought that the shy little nobody in high school would have bodyguards? Certainly not her! But here she was, flanked by two men who were probably armed with a gun of some sort, possibly more than one, and she was stepping into a limousine on her way to be married to a sheik. She had absolutely no idea what that meant for herself. This life was a mystery and she still was having a hard time believing that Dassar would pluck a woman up out of obscurity, someone with no training, no polish and no family ties to recommend her, just so that he could be quickly married. Oh, and produce an heir.

Nope, she couldn't forget that!

As she looked out the window of the limousine, she realized that the whole downtown area seemed deserted. Normally, there were several people walking along the wooden walkways, even Charlie and Norman, the barbers who cut every male head within a six mile radius, should be ensconced outside the barber shop, waiting for customers and chatting or arguing about everything under the sun. But no one was around.

The limousine turned right, away from the town and she had no idea where the driver was taking her. A scary thought occurred to her. What if someone were kidnapping her? What if someone were trying to keep Dassar from fulfilling the terms of the peace treaty?

The idea terrified her so much that she actually leaned forward, about to speak with the driver. But at that same moment, the limousine rounded the corner and there, right before her eyes, was the most romantic gesture anyone could have given her.

Dassar knew that she wasn't happy about this, but instead of just a ceremony in front of a judge that would have sufficed, he had given her a wedding! As she looked out the window, every person from town was standing in front of elegant wooden chairs, smiling at the vehicle as they waited for her to make an appearance. There were flowers everywhere! And at the end of the center aisle was a structure that hadn't been there two days ago. Draped in white, billowy fabric which was tied back at the four corners was a tall gazebo with a table filled with flowers right in the center. And to one side stood Dassar and the town minister waiting for her.

She was literally overwhelmed by the sweet, romantic scene in front of her. When she stepped out of the limousine, cheers from every member of the town greeted her. They were clapping and laughing, delighted with the surprise and excited to be a part of it. One of the little girls raced up and handed her a giant bouquet of flowers and Luna wanted to hide and smile and cheer as well. She couldn't believe that Dassar had done all of this. Or more specifically, he'd ordered someone else to do it. The whole thing was so over the top, she couldn't even speak. She just held the white and soft pink roses and peonies close while she fought the tears that once again threatened.

But then the music started and she brightened up. Ignoring the trembling in her legs and her hands, she walked down the grass pathway towards the beautiful structure, taking Dassar's hands when he reached out for her.

He took her breath away, she thought as she noted his dark suit and silver tie. He looked magnificent! And he was going to be hers? She couldn't believe it. Didn't understand that either. It was so crazy, she just had to pretend that she understood everything that was happening to her.

The minister cleared his throat and everyone took their seats. She tried hard to listen to the words. She really did! But she was so nervous, so worried that she was doing the right thing, that she completely missed the entire service. She glanced back at the people who had served as her family after her arrival here in this town. All of them were thrilled for her, smiling and looking delighted as the ceremony progressed. If she had doubts, their smiling, excited faces somehow reassured her. She owed each of them this wedding, she thought. And everything it would give to them. They'd done so much for her, no questions asked. When she'd arrived in this town nine years ago, this wonderful group of people had adopted her, helped her heal and thrive. This was the only way to protect them, she told herself. She would go through with this and make the best of it all.

If Dassar hadn't squeezed her hands, indicating that it was her turn to promise to love, honor and cherish, she would have continued to stand next to him like some sort of dressed up zombie in a pretty dress.

"I do," she finally said, hearing the chuckles behind her and ignoring them.

The minister turned to Dassar, asking him to promise the same and he spoke easily as he said, "I do."

There was more talking, rings were exchanged then the minister smiled as he said, "I now pronounce you husband and wife." A moment later, the crowd behind her cheered but Luna wasn't sure if she should be happy or sad. She felt both and, strangely, she felt an odd sense of rightness. Even when Dassar turned her so that they were facing each other, placed a hand on each side of her face and bent lower, kissing her in front of everyone, she still felt that this wasn't so horribly wrong.

And even that feeling caused her to panic. This was wrong! This was terribly wrong! She'd just lied in front of God and everyone because she had no idea of she could love this man. He was a stranger who lived in a strange land and she wasn't sure what to do or what to think.

But he'd created a beautiful scene where she could live out one of her dreams…wasn't that worth something? Didn't that mean he cared, just a little bit?

And yes, she had to admit that she cared. Just a little, she thought as she looked into his eyes. She was once again struck by the strange light in his eyes, something that told her that this meant more than just a man purchasing a wife. Could it mean that she was important to him? As more than just a way to meet the requirements of a peace treaty?

Instead of trying to figure it out, she let him turn so that they were facing the crowd as he walked her back down the aisle. Their progress was slow because everyone wanted to give Luna a hug, wish them well and introduce themselves to Dassar. She saw his bodyguards move in closer, their eyes covered by sunglasses but they were still intently watching the crowds. They surrounded the congregation and Dassar realized it as well, tried to move them down the aisle a bit more efficiently.

"Drinks are in the barn!" Hasif called out. The crowd once again cheered, louder this time, but it did the trick. Instead of trying to greet the newlyweds, the congregation moved off in the general direction of the old barn.

Luna had been so overwhelmed by the events of the early afternoon that she hadn't taken the time to look around. Sure enough, the old barn that had been about to fall down was now an elegant, rustic space with more flowers and more of the draping white fabric falling from the rafters in a romantic swirl to the floor. Her heart swelled with a strange feeling as she looked out at all of her friends and neighbors laughing and talking, having a good time.

She stood there, staring at the beautiful reception and smiled, feeling as if the world was okay for a few moments. She hadn't felt this way since this man next to her had walked into her inn several days ago.

No, even before that. There had been so much stress over the debts and the future of the town that things hadn't been happy and relaxed in months. Looking at the members of the town now, they were laughing and cheering, standing in line at the many bars around the room for drinks while sampling the appetizers that were now being circulated by passing waiters.

"We need to have our pictures taken," Dassar rumbled in her ear.

Luna looked up at him, then at the photographer that was standing awkwardly to the side. All of Dassar's bodyguards were in a perimeter around him and she shivered, realizing the threats that this man lived with daily. At this moment, she felt like she was in love with him. He hadn't needed to do this, she thought. He'd arranged all of this for her. She was fairly sure that his purposes would have been fulfilled by a judge and a simple ceremony so she was overwhelmed with gratitude for all of this effort.

She smiled up at him, almost laughing at his startled expression. "Yes, of course." Just like a normal wedding, she thought and stepped over to the picturesque spot where the photographer had already set the stage for some very pretty pictures.

Luna smiled at all the appropriate times while the photographer clicked away. She tried very hard not to feel anything, but Dassar's arms were around her, holding her hand, touching her shoulder. And when the photographer asked for a kiss, she was relieved when Dassar shook his head and denied that request. "We're finished," he stated firmly. Her feelings were all jumbled up right at the moment and a kiss from Dassar was never simple. It would have really thrown her mind a curve ball. As it was, she wanted to stand here in the center of his arms and ignore the rest of the people who were celebrating. She wanted to be near him and feel his strength surrounding her. But at the same time, she wanted to rail at him for being so unfair and unprincipled.

The photographer wanted to argue but he knew when the voice of authority spoke and he stepped back, nodding his head reluctantly.

"Why don't you go and enjoy the reception for a while?" he suggested. "I'm sure your friends are eager to greet you."

She looked up at him, sensing a strange tension in him that she didn't understand. "Aren't you going to join me?" Wasn't that a silly question, she thought. Why in the world would she want to be with him? But there it was. The idea of walking off, of not having his hand holding hers made her feel…bereft.

What an odd thought. So when he shook his head, she was somewhat relieved. "I have to take this phone call."

Luna looked over and realized that Hasif was holding a cell phone against his chest, waiting patiently for Dassar to have a moment.

Luna nodded her head and stepped into the reception area. A glass of something was immediately pressed into her hand but she didn't drink it, not sure how her stomach might react to anything right at the moment. She hadn't been able to eat breakfast or lunch again today, but the reason was much different from the previous day. And she doubted there was anything Dassar could say to get her to eat anything either. Unlike last night, she was too full of nerves now.

What was going to happen next? He'd said he needed to leave. And hadn't he said something about going back to his country with her as his wife? Yes, she doubted that she would be allowed to stay here with her friends. That wouldn't help him get her pregnant.

Oh good grief, she thought with trepidation. The wedding night!

It wasn't that she had ignored it. She just hadn't let herself think about it.

She stood to one side of the barn for several moments, her mind wandering while her eyes took in everyone's happiness. Melanie turned at that moment and realized that Luna looked lost and walked over to her friend. "You okay?" she asked, handing Luna a champagne glass but it wasn't just filled with champagne. Oh no, there couldn't be something so tame as simple champagne at Dassar's wedding! Whoever had organized this had added sparkly, gold sugar crystals to the rim of each champagne glass.

Luna lifted her hand and tasted, surprised by the sharp yet sweet taste. She'd had champagne in the past, but hadn't liked it but this was definitely better! No cheap, sweet champagne for Dassar! His wedding would serve only the best champagne available!

It struck her as odd that she was becoming resentful of the quality of the wine served. What was she really doing? Surely she wasn't becoming angry because Dassar had ordered good champagne? For her? And for the people she cared about?

This day was supposed to be magical and, if her emotions weren't so scattered, she might even enjoy the day. But this sensation that Dassar was...more? That he needed her? And that...perhaps she might need him? Goodness, what was she thinking? She'd been perfectly fine up until now without him in her life. Okay, so there was that irritating problem of her oversized mortgage.

Goodness, she wasn't sure if she was angry, sad, confused, touched or numb. Perhaps a bit of all of the above, she thought. And maybe she had a right to be all of those things. After everything that had happened over the past week, she was exhausted trying to figure things out.

So instead, she was going to relax, have a good time and...yes, she might just get drunk. Perhaps that was the best solution! If she drank enough of this amazing champagne, maybe things would start to make sense. Or maybe, she wouldn't even try to make sense of things.

She sighed even as someone pulled her deeper into the party. There were buffets set up as well as several bars, tables filled with extravagant foods, platters of seafood, elegant appetizer type dishes and sweets that were so beautifully displayed it was almost a shame to touch any of them.

An hour later, she was in a group of people and finally starting to relax. She'd stopped drinking the champagne and had moved to the lemonade, deciding that getting drunk at her own wedding wouldn't be such a great idea. Besides, she wasn't a heavy drinker anyway. She'd tried it once and it was a miserable feeling.

When she felt the tingles along her neck, she knew that Dassar was close. She couldn't believe that he'd been on a phone call for over an hour, but she knew that he hadn't joined in the festivities. She supposed that he might not feel married, not having been married with his country's traditions. So when she looked across the room and their eyes clashed, something happened to her. She wasn't exactly sure what, but there was just a feeling. She remembered that feeling of rightness when she was in his arms before and she supposed this was a similar sensation. Her excitement increased with each step he took. By the time he was right in front of her, she could feel her knees wobbling and her fingers shaking, just as they had that first time she'd seen him.

But as she looked up at him, her excitement was replaced by dread. There was something in his eyes, a look that told her she wasn't going to like whatever it was he was going to say to her.

"We have to leave, Luna," he said into her ear, low enough so only she could hear.

She didn't want to leave. Luna instinctively knew that leaving meant more than just leaving the party. It meant leaving everything. All that she held dear was going to be gone as soon as she stepped away from this party.

She shook her head, trying to deny what he was saying. But his eyes hardened and he nodded ever so slightly. With a grace she didn't know she was capable of, she set the glass of lemonade onto one of the tables. "It's time," she whispered to Melanie.

The woman turned with startled eyes towards her friend. "Time for what?" she asked.

"I have to go." Luna fought the tears. "Will you take over the inn for me?" she asked.

Melanie's smile started to fade. "Take over? What do you mean?"

Luna gripped Melanie's hands. "I have to go with Dassar. I'll call you but can you watch over it until we talk?"

"Of course, darlin'. But you'll still be in charge. Just go and have a great time with your new guy and don't worry about anything. We'll figure out what needs to happen until you're back."

Luna nodded and hugged her friend. "Thanks. Don't let Dorothy sleep too much. And Lucifer comes back every night. Make sure his food bowl is filled but not before six o'clock because then the raccoons get the scent and eat it all up before Lucifer can get anything to eat."

She wiped a tear from her eye. "Oh, and Barry knows all about the chickens. He'll take care of them. But you have to get their eggs right after breakfast. Otherwise, they will peck your hands."

Melanie laughed. "Just go, honey! We'll take care of everything! You'll be fine!"

Luna was very scared that she'd never see these people again. She hugged them all as she walked with Dassar towards the waiting limousine. She appreciated his patience as she said goodbye to everyone, all these people who had adopted her when she'd moved here so long ago. If only…

There was no good reason to go down that path. It led to nothing productive so she gave one more hug to Norman a moment before she stepped into the limousine. The door closing felt like her heart was breaking but she wouldn't let the tears fall. She couldn't.

Dassar saw her wounded look and he wanted to put the smile back into her eyes. She was a beautiful woman, but he hated it when she looked sad as she did at the moment. "You'll be back, Luna."

Her eyes widened with those words. "I will?"

"Yes. You can visit often if you'd like."

She was so relieved that she could visit her friends that she actually threw herself into his arms. "Oh, thank you!" she gasped. "Goodness, I thought I would never see most of those people again."

He laughed softly, relieved to have her in his arms again. She felt so good and her soft, silken arms were around his neck. It seemed perfectly natural to lean down and kiss the delicate shell of her ear.

She moaned with the brief caress, but caught herself just in time. "What are you doing?" she demanded, pulling back as far as he would let her go.

He chuckled. "It has been too long if you are questioning what I was doing."

She shivered and tried to scoot back onto her seat. "I don't think…" that horrible trembling that she hated so much started up again full force. "We shouldn't…"

Dassar wanted to laugh but she just looked so serious. And sexy as hell. Damn it, the woman was in her wedding dress and trying to tell him that she didn't want him to touch her!

"We're going to make love, Luna. Count on it."

She shook her head and scooted off of his lap, relieved that he allowed her to move back onto the soft, leather seat. "Dassar, we really shouldn't."

"We really should. We discussed this, Luna."

She scooted further to her side of the limousine. "Yes, but couldn't we just hold off on that part of our relationship? I mean, we don't know each other very well and it would be nice to…" she stopped speaking when she saw the laughter in his eyes. "You're not going to agree to this, are you?" she asked with irritation. He had been so sweet and wonderful today and then, when he'd told her that she could come back and visit, she'd thought he was starting to become human again. Or at least someone who wasn't the horrible, arrogant ruler that she'd initially met.

He leaned forward and took her fingers in a loose hold. "I'll make a deal with you," he offered, pulling her closer slightly. "We won't make love again until you are ready."

The words were nice, but she sensed an underlying message that she wasn't quite sure about. "What's the catch?" she asked.

He turned her hand over, his thumb tracing patterns on the palm. "No catch. You tell me when you are ready and I will be right there, more than ready to accommodate your needs."

She watched him for a long moment, still not sure what he wasn't telling her. But she had no alternative but to go along with the offer. "You'll respect my decision when I say no?"

He shrugged one of those enormous, muscular shoulders. "I won't like it. But I'll respect your wishes." A smile grew on those hard, firm lips. "And I reserve the right to try and change your mind."

Luna's breath caught in her throat. There was the catch! Goodness, the heat that filled her was like lava flowing quickly through her veins. No longer was the touch on her palm just erotic. It was a promise! And an invitation.

# Chapter 8

The limousine purred to a stop right on the tarmac where a large, private plane was waiting, stairs in place and a uniformed flight attendant standing at attention at the top. Dassar held her hand as they moved out of the limousine and she felt decidedly silly as she walked up the stairs in her voluminous wedding dress.

"We'll be upstairs," he told Hasif as soon as they stepped onto the plane. The plane was actually filled with people. Not just the bodyguards she'd already met but a whole staff of personnel who were busy working on whatever it was they worked on. Luna only had a brief glimpse of the crowd as they started to settle down into the various seats of the plane. It wasn't like a commercial plane although it was definitely an enormous jumbo jet but only part of the main cabin had seats like a normal plane. The rest looked like small areas to congregate and all of the seats were larger, more comfortable. She'd never flown before but she'd read numerous articles about how cramped commercial planes were.

This plane and the comfortable seats were the exact opposite of a commercial flight. Everything seemed to be designed for the utmost comfort and maximum space so that each person had enough space to work and spread out easily.

Dassar took her up a set of winding stairs to the upper level and Luna discovered that this area was more like a living room with elegant tables and chairs, a bar in one corner and even a conference room taking over one end.

"Is this seat okay?" he asked solicitously.

She looked around, stunned anew by signs of Dassar's wealth. "This is fine," she whispered, not sure what to say. She slipped into the seat, trying to get comfortable. But she was still in her wedding dress, she was terrified of where they were heading and not sure about Dassar or what her life would be like in the next twenty-four hours.

"You look like someone is about to jump out and do something horrible to you," he said as a staff member approached.

"All the letters are ready, Your Highness," the man said, holding a stack of envelopes.

Dassar took the stack and flipped through them before handing them to Luna. "Would you like to look through these?" he asked. "See if there are any that we missed?"

Dassar knew that none were missing. These were the letters releasing all of the town's people from their debts. He hadn't just extended their payment terms as she'd originally requested. He'd wiped out their debts. He'd also had his staff go through their financials and figure out ways to improve each person's business and a letter was included with that advice. "I have a business representative coming to the town tomorrow to help the business owners with future plans. That should help them to stay out of debt."

Her eyes snapped up to his, astonished with his generosity. "That's very kind of you," she said self-consciously. She bit her lip, thinking that was an amazing wedding present. But she couldn't stifle the feeling that she'd just been bought and paid for with these letters.

She handed the stack back to the man standing stiffly beside Dassar, not sure what else to say. Luna felt both happy and humiliated about these letters.

Dassar quickly understood where her mind was going and he wasn't going to let herself think that way. "You are helping to secure the future of so many people, Luna. Not just the people in your town, but also the people in my country. They are going to love you. Already, the news has come out and they are eager to meet you."

Luna smiled weakly, not sure if she could live up to anyone's expectations. "Dassar, this is crazy. I'm not the kind of person that can make this kind of relationship work. I'm not good with crowds or strangers. I was the shy one in school. I was the one that liked to be in the background."

Taking the letters, he handed them back to the staff member and then nodded to dismiss him. When they were once again alone, he sat down and looked at her. "You're my wife now. How do you feel?"

Luna wasn't sure what she was thinking or feeling right now. She licked her lips, unaware of the way Dassar's eyes zeroed in on her tongue or the fullness of her lips. "So much has happened in the past few days, I don't think I've processed anything yet. I mean," she looked around at the stunning luxury surrounding her and suddenly realized that the plane was in the air. "We're flying?!" she gasped and looked back at Dassar. "We're in the air?"

"Yes. The pilot was only waiting for the two of us."

She looked towards the front of the plane as if she could see through the walls to the pilots in the cockpit. "But, when did we take off?"

"Only a few moments ago."

She shook her head, still not sure what was going on. "This is all so crazy," she sighed and sat back in her chair, rubbing her forehead. "I can't believe I'm married," she whispered. Her hand suddenly felt heavy and she looked at it, seeing the heavy rings for the first time. One was a wide gold band and the other held an enormous diamond ring. She stared, not sure when they'd been placed on her hand. They looked strange against her fingers, almost foreign.

"You don't remember me putting those rings on your finger, do you?" he asked.

Luna's mouth went slack. "No. Not really."

"Do you remember promising to love, honor and obey me?"

Luna's humor came alive with that comment. "Obey? What else are you going to command me to do?"

Dassar looked at the woman in her beautiful gown that made her waist look impossibly small and her breasts fuller, her hips and slender legs were all perfect. "Oh, I can think of several things I'd like to command you to do," he commented with a roguish look in his dark eyes. He couldn't stop the amusement from coming out when she blushed and looked down, unable to hold his gaze. For all intents and purposes, this woman was still innocent and he couldn't wait to show her more about sexuality and the pleasures of the bedroom. They'd had only a few hours together. And there was so much more that she could learn. So much more that he wanted to teach her.

Reaching down, he lifted her leg, placing it on his knee. Startled and not sure what he was doing, Luna tried to pull her leg away. But his hand held her foot firmly on his lap and his eyes glanced up at her. "Breaking your vows already, eh?"

Her mouth was dry as his long fingers slipped her satin shoe off of her foot. "Pastor Jim eliminated 'obey' from his vows a long time ago. There was an uproar in the community about it but he held firm. He changed it to 'cherish'."

He smiled slightly, but wasn't put off. "And are you going to love, honor and cherish me, Luna?"

She realized that Dassar had slipped her beautiful shoe off and his strong thumbs and fingers were pressing against the arch of her foot. What she thought should feel relaxing was anything but. The way his fingers and thumb were moving against the muscles in her foot, sparks of something crazy were shooting straight up her leg, ending at the apex of her legs and she jerked her leg, but he'd been anticipating that and held her firm still. "Does it feel good?" he asked, sliding his hands higher up her legs, massaging her calf muscle. "Tell me what you like, Luna."

She suppressed a moan with his touch and gripped the armrests of her chair, trying hard not to fall under his spell. "You know I don't know what I like," she whispered, wanting to curl up into a ball of shame because he could reduce her to an aching, quivering ball of need so easily.

She closed her eyes and held her breath as she said, "Please, don't do this to me. Not here. Not right now," she asked of him.

Dassar looked at the woman who was practically writhing in the seat and relented. "Not here. And not now," he agreed. "But soon."

She pulled her foot away and slipped her shoe back onto her foot. "Can you tell me a bit about your country? What you do and what to expect when we…" she struggled over any more words. She was so overwhelmed by the idea of what she might be facing, her fear was making her lips numb.

Dassar saw the anxiety in her eyes and he didn't like it. He had people down on the lower level who were waiting for him, issues that needed his direction and his insight, but he ignored all of those responsibilities and started talking to her. He told her about the majestic mountains of Altair, the people and the culture, about his family who already knew about her and were eager to meet her. He kept on talking, noting the way she released her seat belt and curled her legs up underneath her as she listened intently. Luna asked questions and he answered them, trying to give her as much information as he could without adding to her unease.

Dinner was served and, after she changed into comfortable clothes, he was relieved that she ate more food now, suspecting that she hadn't eaten any breakfast because she had been too busy preparing food for him and his men. And he knew she hadn't eaten lunch or anything at the reception besides champagne and lemonade. He might have been on the phone dealing with a border crisis, but he'd kept his eye on her, wanting to feast his eyes on the beautiful woman who had become his wife.

As he continued to talk, he was surprised at the feeling of possessiveness that had come over him after the minister announced that Luna Montgomery was his wife. She was now Luna bin Sarook and his chest swelled with pride and some other strange sensation he wasn't willing to investigate too closely.

When her exhaustion started to catch up with her, he carried her into the back of the plane and laid her down on the bed, taking off her shoes and the simple dress she'd donned. His body hardened painfully when he saw the underwear that she was wearing. The corset pushed up her breasts, filling the cups to overflowing. The delicate lace of her underwear perfectly matched the lace at the top of her thigh high stockings.

If he'd known what she was wearing underneath that dress, he never would have been able to concede to her desire to wait. They would have been back here all this time and he would have helped her lose her anxiety through the pleasure their bodies could give to each other.

With a sigh that sounded suspiciously like a groan, he covered her up and walked out of the bedroom.

# Chapter 9

Luna gripped Dassar's hand as if it were a lifeline. She couldn't believe the huge crowd of men and women that were waiting at the entrance to the palace to greet them. "What's going on?" she asked, pressing her side against his strong body. She didn't like feeling as if she needed his protection, but she wasn't going to give it up and try to look strong right now. She was terrified and confused. She'd woken up on the plane less than fifteen minutes before it was supposed to land. She was now wearing a pretty yellow suit that made her feel incredibly feminine. There were even matching shoes, but nothing could prepare her to face a crowd of this size.

All of her teenage shyness came roaring back to life and she wanted to bury her face in Dassar's chest. Instead, she forced herself to look at the crowd, to smile as several people stepped forward to greet both of them. She had absolutely no idea what they were saying and was relieved when one man in particular switched to English, hopefully repeating what the other person just said.

"You are a beautiful flower and we are all thrilled that you have graced us with your loveliness," the shorter man said, handing her a bouquet of flowers with a very deep bow.

Luna held onto the flowers, her hands almost hurting as her anxiety increased over this unexpected presentation. "That's very kind of you," she replied, hoping that she was saying the right thing.

Dassar leaned down and told her, "The ladies of my family will take care of you now. Don't be afraid, okay? They'll help you through the next few hours."

Luna wanted to ask him what he meant, but two of the ladies were taking her hands and leading her away. She looked back at Dassar, her eyes pleading with him to explain, or even better, to save her from this new confusion.

Several hours later, Luna could not believe what her body had gone through. She'd been nudged into a shower and was told in broken English to use a special soap. When she'd finished with that, she was led out to a table where her body was scrubbed with a loofah everywhere. She felt painfully self-conscious when the woman doing the scrubbing even scrubbed her breasts and her private parts. When the brusque servant started to go through another round with that loofah thing, Luna shook her head. The woman tried to explain that it was okay but Luna was definitely not okay with that. It was torture!

Next was a massage where her entire body was oiled and rubbed and massaged to the point where she felt like a battered piece of chicken. Why women paid to have this, Luna didn't understand. After that, she was nudged back into the shower and more lavender soap, lavender shampoo and lavender conditioner.

After each treatment, she looked around, trying to find some way to escape but there were so many women receiving the same treatment and no apparent exit areas. Or at least none she could reach easily.

The scrubbing treatment had been a piece of cake compared to what came next. Apparently shaving wasn't good enough. She'd shaved her legs and armpits this morning, or was it yesterday morning? She had no idea what day it was or even what time it was.

A woman came forward with a big bowl of hot wax and Luna cringed. But she allowed the ladies to wax her legs, her armpits and… "No!" she stated emphatically when the woman started to wax her private area. She scooted back from the lady who was trying to do her job, shaking her head. The woman was very kind though and explained in very broken English, "Not hurt as bad as think."

Luna didn't believe her but she was willing to give it a try. And then she found out that the lady lied! Oh goodness did she lie! Luna screamed when the wax was ripped off of her, her eyes wide and angry now. The lady only laughed and applied a soothing cream, shaking her head and winking at Luna. "Funny," she said before disappearing. A robe was brought out to her and Luna gratefully slipped the material over her naked body. She'd never been naked for so long, nor had she ever been in a situation where strangers would see her naked body! It was strange and disconcerting that so many of the women thought this was perfectly natural.

Luna sighed as two more women approached, one for a manicure and another for a pedicure. This was nice, she thought, but then someone else came behind her and started to do something to her hair. Bam! Back was all of her confusion. And good grief, yet one more person came over and started a manicure on her other hand! She almost laughed out loud when a fifth servant came and started on her second foot. There were five people working on her at the same time! This was insanity and she couldn't stop the laugh that bubbled up.

Unfortunately, her laughter caused everyone else in the room to stop what they were doing and look at her. Some of the older women looked decidedly disapproving and she smothered her panicked laughter and apologized. A moment later, everyone was back to work, more chattering and chaos, more servants appeared and started working on other ladies and everyone seemed to pick up the pace for some reason.

Luna kept looking around, wishing that someone would explain to her what was going on, but they were all hurrying around. When a makeup person started in on Luna's face, she gave in, not even trying to understand any longer. She supposed that someone would explain it to her at some point. But right now, no one seemed to speak English. She came to the realization that she would need to learn this language fast! Otherwise, she would be swallowed up by beauty treatments and confusion and she'd die of being smothered by...well, she had no idea what was being smeared all over her face. It was so thick, she felt as if she was wearing a mask!

A gorgeous red and gold robe-like dress was brought forward after her makeup and hair was judged acceptable by two of the older, more authoritative looking women of the group. The silky robe was taken from her and Luna's arms came up, trying to cover up her nakedness once more. But before she could pull on the exotic robe, she was given the sheerest robe she'd ever seen. There really was no reason to wear such an item but she was told through hand gestures to put it on. Where was a bra when a gal needed one, she thought? And how about a pair of underwear! Good grief, what she would do for her Bugs Bunny underwear! It was soft and comfortable and at least part of her body would be covered up by something. Anything! She was naked here! Good grief.

The red and gold robe was brought forward along with a gorgeous pair of red shoes. Thankfully, these weren't too high, and they were comfortable. The robe was tied around her waist and a mirror was brought closer so she could see herself.

Luna stared at the woman in the mirror, wondering who she was. There was so much makeup on her face, her blue eyes surrounded by liner that was so thick, her eyes appeared to be enormous. She was wearing a lipstick that perfectly matched the red of the gown but Luna had never in her life worn this color of lipstick. She didn't think it would go with her complexion but since her whole face and neck were covered with muck, her complexion was hidden.

And her hair! Good grief, her blond hair was piled up on top of her head with little diamonds and gold coins tucked in. The coins jingled if she moved even slightly!

The ladies were urging her forward once again so Luna walked, wondering what could possibly be next.

The doors, and escape, were finally opened. Unfortunately, escape was not an option. The ladies were lined up behind her and, when she peered through the doors, she was greeted by an entire room filled with men. Every eye was upon her and she stood frozen in place, not sure what to do.

So when Dassar stepped forward, taking her hand and leading her forward, she almost sobbed with relief. But she didn't dare. She was too afraid of what might happen to her makeup if she spilled even one tear during this whole baffling process.

Dassar looked at the woman on his arm and wanted to laugh but knew that his Luna was holding on by a very fine thread. He should have warned her about what was going to happen, but he'd gotten distracted by his staff. The next thing he knew, his pretty wife was being taken away by his relatives.

At least, he thought this was his wife. He'd tried to hide the surprise on his face when the doors had opened up but the woman standing in the doorway didn't much resemble his wife. Her white-blond hair was the same, and this woman had blue eyes, but everything else about her was…different!

The Altair wedding ceremony proceeded along and Dassar spoke at the appropriate times. When it was her turn, he squeezed her fingers, getting her to look up at him. With a few jingles from her hair, she turned to look at him and he told her slowly what she should say. She quickly repeated the words and he was proud of her. She looked completely out of her element but she was dealing with all of the surprises extremely well.

A moment later, they were once again pronounced married and Dassar turned to kiss her. He wasn't exactly sure where to kiss her though. The makeup was so thick on her face. But he also saw that she was blinking back tears and so he moved closer and kissed her gently on her overly red lips. "It's going to be okay," he promised her, squeezing her hands since no other touch would be appropriate at this point.

He turned and tucked her hand onto his arm, then raised his own arm to greet the guests, all of whom jumped up and cheered at the announcement that their ruler was now a married man.

"We'll have a feast and then it will all be over. Can you make it?" he asked, leaning his dark head down to hers so she didn't have to move too much.

"I can make it. Can you tell me what time it is though?"

He wasn't exactly sure what time it was, but he said, "It is around lunch time."

"And the day?" she asked, thinking of her perfectly soft, day-of-the-week underwear that would feel so comfortable right about now. Good grief, any kind of underwear would be comfortable at this moment!

"It is Saturday."

Luna nodded, then stopped moving her head because she was too afraid that her hair would topple from the weight of all of the diamonds and coins. "Good to know," she sighed.

He led her to the reception area and seated her at the head table right next to him. From that point on, food was brought out, one platter after another. There was so much food and Dassar put a small amount on the plate both of them were apparently going to share during the meal.

After what seemed like hours, with food coming in and going out, numerous speeches and toasts, all of which Dassar translated for her, the clapping started.

Luna had absolutely no idea what the clapping meant, but she was relieved when Dassar stood up and led her out of the room.

When they were finally out of the banquet room, she looked around and sighed with relief that there was no longer an audience watching her every move. "Is it over?" she asked as quietly as she could with so many guards in the hallway.

Dassar chuckled. "Yes. It is finally over. You are again my wife."

"Hm…" she said, still not moving her head. "Good to know."

Dassar laughed as he opened an elaborately decorated set of double doors, both of which were closed behind them.

"Are we finally alone?" she asked, not moving her head even to turn from side to side in order to investigate her new surroundings.

"Yes. We are alone," he told her, his voice turning husky now that he was allowed to make love to his wife.

"Thank goodness!" she sighed.

And then she did something Dassar never would have anticipated. With deft fingers and a lot of jingling, she bent her head and tore at the belt of her wedding robe. A moment later, the robe fell to the floor and Dassar's mouth went dry as he watched his wife step out of the shoes, out of the robe and walk towards the only other open doorway which led to the bathroom. "I'm washing my face," she told him in a tone that wouldn't allow any argument.

Not that Dassar would say a word to that plan. He couldn't speak. He was too busy watching his wife walk through his bedroom in nothing but a sheer robe that hid absolutely nothing from his eyes, although all he could see at the moment was her adorable bottom as she disappeared into his bathroom.

Their bathroom now, he reminded himself.

It took her so long in the bathroom, he couldn't contain his curiosity. He had already stripped off his tunic and was unbuttoning his shirt when he stopped in the doorway. His little wife had discarded the diaphanous robe and was now wearing his enormous silk robe. The robe he almost never wore but his servants continued to put out onto the hook for him. The silk was dark blue and huge on her, but he suspected that the shy little woman was feeling better now that she was covered up with something. Not that he was going to allow her to keep it on for much longer.

He watched with fascination as she rubbed soap on her delicate features, amused at how much makeup was coming off. "How much did you put on?" he asked with a chuckle.

She glared at him, but it wasn't very effective since the area around her eyes was mostly black now. "I didn't put any makeup on myself. Apparently, I'm not trained well enough to put my own makeup on. I had five people," she paused to raise a soapy hand with all of her fingers spread out to emphasize her point. "Five! All of them doing my nails, toes, hair and makeup. It was crazy!"

He laughed softly when the soap slipped lower and she had to close her eyes and rinse off the soap. But she didn't stop there. Apparently, she needed multiple wash cycles in order to get it all off. It was even on her neck, he realized, noting that the neckline of his robe was wet because she was trying to wash it all off.

When she finally lifted her head and reached for a towel, she was back to the woman he'd met several days ago, in all of her soft, natural beauty. He had to admit that he much preferred this woman to the one with all of the crazy makeup on. He'd have to tell his mother that he never wanted to see Luna looking so different in the future. He liked her like this. She was fresh and lovely, alive! And he could see her blue eyes much more easily.

"Wow! That was a crazy morning," she said and walked out of the bathroom, the blue silk robe trailing on the floor behind her.

Dassar's eyebrow went up as his new wife once again walked out on him. He was leaning against the bathroom countertop, his arms crossed over his chest as he contemplated his next move.

But in the end, the image of Luna stepping out of her wedding finery in that see-through robe flashed into his mind. With that image in his head, there was nothing that could stop him from making love to his wife. So with a determined stride, he walked out, only to find Luna frozen, staring at his enormous bed. It was round, surrounded by sheer curtains that were pulled back at the moment. Around that bed was a circle of columns that separated the sleeping area from the rest of his suite. But the suite's entire focus was that bed. And all of Dassar's focus was on what he was going to do in that bed.

Sweeping Luna up into his arms, he carried her over to the bed. His shirt was already unbuttoned, so when he laid her down, he stood up and ripped off the shirt. He left his pants on, but only because his gentle wife looked terrified. They had made love before, but that had been in her inn where she felt more comfortable. Looking at her now, he knew that he would have to slow down. As much as he wanted to ravish this woman in so many ways, she needed to be cared for. She'd been thrown into a situation where she'd had almost no information on what was happening and she'd come through it beautifully.

Now he needed to do the same.

So he leaned over her, an arm on both sides of her, and he kissed her. As gently as he could, he seduced his wife. When he felt her lips soften, only then did he lower his bare chest to her silk covered body.

For a long time, he didn't do anything other than kiss her and hold her in his arms. But as she softened more, his hands started to explore. He kept things slow and easy, not wanting to overwhelm her just yet, but his hands carefully pulled the blue silk away so that his eyes could feast on her perfect body. When his mouth latched onto her breast, he loved the way she moved against him, making those sexy sounds that he remembered from the last time he'd had her in his arms.

When she came alive, her hands smoothed down his body and he had to grit his teeth as need surged through him. Her tiny hands had been pampered today and were so soft and smooth, it drove him crazy. Even her short nails looked sexy as hell against his darker skin.

"Do that again," he told her and showed her how he liked to be touched.

Luna was fascinated by this man and all of the surprising textures on his body. The last time they'd been together, everything had been fast and furious. There hadn't been enough time to explore, to let her fingers just roam over the surface of his body. But he was letting her now and she loved it. Not that she hadn't thoroughly enjoyed the last time. Well, she'd enjoyed it until it had ended and her mind could focus on the reality of what she'd done.

But she wasn't going to let herself think about that now. Reality was far away and she was making this moment, this time with the man who was now her husband, her reality. So when his lips captured her nipple, bringing his teeth and his tongue into play, she couldn't stop her back arching, offering him more. And this reality was very nice!

Luna's fingers dove into his hair, loving the feel of the soft strands between her fingers. She suspected that this was the only part of Dassar that was soft.

His mouth moved lower and she smiled, relieved that he was no longer torturing her breasts. But when he moved even lower, she realized what he was about to do. "No Dassar," she begged, shifting her hips so that she was out of reach.

Dassar almost laughed, but he was too intent on tasting this woman and finding out more of her secrets. "Ah, Luna," he chuckled softly as he grabbed her hips and pulled her right back to him. "Do you really think you can get away from me?" He didn't wait for an answer, but he lifted himself up on his arms and kissed her. Gone was the tenderness, the gentle seduction. This kiss was absolute possession. He was claiming her and her body responded.

When he lifted his head, he looked into her blue eyes and said, "Don't move, Luna," and he went right back to his goal.

Of course, Luna wasn't going to take that and she sat up, trying to stop him but he only laughed and held her still while his mouth claimed her once again.

Luna slammed back against the mattress, her whole mind going blank as her world exploded from the touch of his mouth on her core. His tongue and his mouth were magical and she had no concept of anything other than the blinding pleasure he was giving her.

When he finally allowed her to come down from that orgasm, he moved right into place, pushing himself fully into her body and she wrapped her legs around him as her body adjusted to his size.

"You're my wife," he growled and she opened her eyes in time to see the look of possession as he looked down at her. She didn't have time to argue with him about that because he started moving and that friction caused her to gasp and grab onto his shoulders. And he shifted, sliding in and out of her, driving her crazy with each thrust. She wanted to scream out but she couldn't make a sound.

Dassar watched, moving and shifting to make it better for her. He was on the edge though, trying very hard to control his own release because she felt so incredibly good right now. So when she spun out over the cliff, he was more than happy to tumble right along with her.

The sensation of feeling her orgasm around him only intensified his own and he was stunned by the power of his climax. When he was finally able to see straight, he pulled himself off of her slender body, but dragged her right along with him. Normally, he preferred to get out of bed and shower immediately after sex. But the thought of moving any muscle in his body, much less losing touch with this woman, was simply not going to happen. He wanted her close but he wasn't going to examine the reasons why. He just did.

# Chapter 10

Luna woke up feeling like someone was watching her. Sliding against the satin soft sheets, she tried to wake up, but her body ached and she wanted Dassar. Wanting to make love with him again despite the soreness between her legs should be wrong, but she didn't care that her body was tender from the last twenty-four hours. She realized that she was addicted to his touch, to the way he made her feel.

But when her arms reached out and found nothing but sheets, she opened her eyes. Only to find herself looking at a very pretty woman who was staring back at her.

Luna yelped and jerked backwards, using the sheet to cover herself up. "I'm sorry, but who are you?" She forgot that most people didn't speak English.

Thankfully, this woman did and she smiled, adding in a curtsy. "I'm your personal maid, Your Highness," she said and lifted the pink fabric that had been draped over her arm.

Luna realized that the woman was holding up a robe made of the most beautiful silk she'd ever seen. "A personal maid?" she repeated, sliding to the edge of the enormous bed but still holding the sheet in front of her. She'd had enough nakedness in front of strangers before her second wedding to last her a lifetime.

"Yes, Your Highness. My name is Reyna and I will help you with anything you need."

Luna pushed her arms into the sleeves of the robe and tied it before she would release the sheet. "That is very kind of you Reyna, but I'm not sure I need a personal servant."

The woman's smile dimmed ever so slightly. "Would you like some tea while I give you a list of my duties? You may add anything to the list that you need."

Luna realized that she'd hurt the woman's feelings. "Tea?" she asked, perking up at that. Tea that she didn't have to make in the morning? "Tea would be wonderful," she said and sighed at the thought of a jolt of caffeine.

Reyna's smile once more brightened and she disappeared for a moment, only to push in a coffee and tea service complete with espresso machine. "What kind of tea would you like?" she asked.

Luna had no idea what to ask. "Just a plain cup of tea?" she suggested.

Reyna immediately went to work. Obviously a plain cup of tea wasn't as simple as it might seem. But the whole time, Reyna listed out all of her duties which included ensuring that Luna's clothes were clean and pressed, that they were tagged appropriately, the room is cleaned and…the list went on and on. Luna had no idea why her clothes needed to be tagged or any of the other numerous tasks Reyna listed out, but it sounded very complicated.

Reyna turned and handed Luna a cup of tea and she took a sip, closing her eyes at how wonderful it tasted. "Oh goodness, this is fabulous. Thank you!"

Reyna nodded happily. "Are you ready to join the spas today? The ladies were all excited that you didn't join them yesterday."

Luna's eyes popped open. "Spas?" she asked, wary of the treatment she'd had before the wedding ceremony. And there was absolutely no way she was going through that waxing stuff again. Maybe on her legs, but…Luna realized that she had stubble in areas that really shouldn't have to endure stubble!

Reyna nodded eagerly. "We saw that His Highness has left for his office so the ladies are eager to show you the spas today. I can accompany you and translate, if you'd like."

Luna thought that would be a great idea. "Thank you for that," she said with feeling. "And is there any way you could teach me the language?"

Reyna smiled brightly. "It would be my honor, but we can also engage a tutor for you as well."

That sounded heavenly.

Her world seemed to be brightening, except for the fact that she'd gone through two marriage ceremonies to a man who, unfortunately, she suspected she was falling in love with but he showed no such emotions coming back to her. She still couldn't believe how sweet and romantic Dassar had been during that first ceremony. It all seemed like some sort of dream. And he was much more generous than he needed to be. Since they both had to go through a second ceremony, she was doubly touched that he would go through the time and expense of marrying her in her own hometown. That had all been for her.

She supposed that yesterday had been for him, but she smiled as she thought about how much she'd enjoyed the day as well. In fact…well, she shook her head as she walked to the bathroom, her body's tenderness coming out as she walked and she had to admit that another day alone with Dassar probably wasn't the best idea.

Although it would have been nice to just be with him. They didn't always have to have sex. Then again, Dassar had a whole country to run. It wasn't like he could just skip out and have a fun time sightseeing. He was the ruler, after all.

As she followed Reyna through the palace, Luna discovered special hallways that lead directly to the spas so that she didn't even need to dress if she didn't want to. Luna heard that comment, but she was so absorbed in trying to figure out how to deal with a marriage without love that she didn't quite understand.

Until she entered the "spa"!

Goodness, she'd thought she'd seen naked before that second wedding. She quickly discovered that her wedding day was nothing! Everyone in this room, except for the servants, was naked. There were about twenty women, all wandering in and out of the pool area where different kinds of jets were massaging muscles. There were still-water pools that Reyna explained were heated to different temperatures. There was a warm one at eighty-five degrees, then a one hundred degree pool and yet another one heated to one hundred and four degrees. After visiting each of those, it was explained that she should plunge into the sixty degree pool to refresh herself, then start all over, or go into the large pool and relax in front of one of the powerful jets. There were jets for the upper back, lower back, shoulders, feet and bottom area.

Luna's eyes skimmed over all of the naked ladies wandering around the various pools, stunned and more than a little intimidated. "And if I don't want to do any of the jets or hot water areas?"

"Oh, then you can relax in the saunas!" she explained with excitement. "There are two different saunas, one with dry heat and one with steam. Choose whichever you prefer."

Luna watched as two ladies giggled while they stepped, naked, into the steam room. Looking around the large, tiled area, she saw that every woman was simply relaxing back against the jets, sitting in one of the heated waters or going into the saunas. There was another door to the back of the room and Luna pointed to it. "What's back there?" she asked, hoping it was an exit to something more clothing related.

Reyna smiled and led the way. "That is for the beauty treatments. You experienced those the other day. If there is any treatment you desire, it can be done for you there."

Luna clutched the robe closer to her, feeling very self-conscious. Many of the women were staring at her, some even waving for her to come into the water.

"Reyna, could you explain to them that I'm fascinated, but still sore?"

Reyna smiled and moved over to one of the ladies. After the explanation, that woman giggled and moved to the next who also laughed, shaking her head. Luna couldn't understand what was so amusing, but she thought back to her words. "No!" she gasped. "I meant I was sore from the last time I went through the treatments!" she told Reyna.

The woman only laughed. Obviously, everyone in the room now thought she was sore because of all the sex she'd had over the past twenty-four hours with their ruler and Luna's face turned bright red.

"The warm water will help you with that," Reyna explained, tugging Luna's robe off and urging her to enter the water.

Luna did so, but mostly because the water would cover up her nakedness. The ladies were all very kind to her, some of them trying to teach her their language and learning how to say things in English as well. There were so many ladies and children, all of whom seemed content to spend the day in the spas, moving from the sauna to the waters, plunging into the cold water then starting all over again. By four o'clock, she was urged into the beauty room and the lady with the hot wax was standing, waiting in ambush. Luna put her foot down at another waxing treatment but she allowed the beauticians to do another manicure and pedicure. She insisted on a robe though and was relieved when one was brought to her. She had no idea why she needed her nails redone but she endured the treatment, smiling appreciatively when the ladies finished and waited for her approval.

When she stepped back into their suite that evening, she was presented with an entire wardrobe of new clothes. She sighed with happiness as she pulled on a bra and underwear set even though there were no cartoon characters or days of the week on any of them. She was just grateful to be dressed finally. She hadn't had a pair of underwear or a bra on for over forty-eight hours and it felt marvelous to be properly clothed once again.

She selected a soft pair of slacks and a knit shirt, still not sure what was going to happen next.

But a few minutes later, she was led to the dining area and Dassar was already there, holding a glass filled with something and his eyes heated up as soon as she stepped into the room.

"Good evening, my lovely wife," he said, handing her the glass filled with something strange.

"What's this?" she asked, sniffing it, afraid of drinking anything else. She'd been plied with liquids and decadent foods all day long. She was going to gain about twenty pounds if she kept eating foods like that and lounging around the pool, doing nothing to exercise her body.

"I believe it is our version of lemonade," he told her.

She looked at his glass. "What are you drinking?"

He chuckled. "I have scotch."

Luna clunked her glass down on the table and took his out of his hands. "Thanks," she said a moment before she lifted the glass to her lips and swallowed the entire amount. She hissed as the heat stole down her throat, closing her eyes. But once the burn ended, she could feel the heat steal through her whole body and she felt better. More in control.

Dassar watched and his body reacted. Damn, she looked beautiful, even when she was stealing his drink. "Better?" he asked, pouring two more glasses of the potent drink, handing one to her.

"Yes," she said. "I hope there is going to be something nutritious for dinner," she said. "And that's saying a lot for me. I love sweets, but I don't think I can live off of sweets for the entire day."

"What did you do today?" he asked as they sat down for dinner. Immediately, the doors were opened and servants stepped into the room, placing food in front of each of them.

Luna looked down at her plate and sighed with happiness. Vegetables! Normally, she would ignore them because they were horrible but right now, her vitamin starved body craved them. Oh, and lean protein! What a treat!

She picked up her knife and fork, her body starving for something that wasn't drenched in honey or nuts. "Why don't you tell me what you did today?" she countered. "I'm pretty sure that my day wasn't as interesting."

He proceeded to tell her about the meetings he'd sat through, the arguments about all sorts of politics and various schemes to increase the economy that were tossed around. "So not very interesting," he told her.

Luna was cutting into very tender, very tasty chicken and smiled. "Oh, I don't know. It seems much more interesting than sitting around the spa all day long. I got the color of my nail polish changed," she said, lifting her hand so that he could see that her nails were pink now instead of red. "That's about all I accomplished."

"And is that a bad thing?" he asked.

Luna lifted her eyes to him. "Did I mention that I was naked all day long?"

He chuckled. "Sounds perfect."

"Surrounded by other naked women!" she amended, her eyebrows going up into her hairline as she tried to get him to understand what a day in the "spa" meant.

Dassar smiled still, not sure where she was going. "You're exciting me, Luna. Perhaps we should change the subject?" he offered.

Luna leaned forward. "Your mother was naked with me. Your grandmother was naked with me, Dassar," she emphasized. "Your great aunts and aunts, all sitting around naked."

Dassar's smile quickly disappeared to be replaced by a horrified cringe. "Okay, that's not very exciting."

"Exactly!" she stated emphatically, pointing her knife in his direction. Her shoulders sagged as she twirled her fork. "Dassar, I can't spend my days sitting around having my nails painted."

He looked across the table at her carefully. "What do you want to do?" he asked.

She pondered the question. "I don't know, to be honest with you. All of this has happened so quickly, I haven't really figured out anything. But the First Lady always chooses one or two issues to really focus on during her time in the White House. Would you mind if I tried to find at least one issue?"

He shook his head. "I'm sorry, but that probably isn't very safe."

Luna considered him for a moment. "But you focus on a lot of issues every day."

"Yes, but when I leave the palace, I am surrounded by guards and I know how to protect myself in a battle."

She bit her lower lip as she thought through his comment. "What about if I learned to protect myself?" she asked. "I don't know much about self-defense, but I could learn."

He carefully placed his fork down on the side of his plate. "I will not allow you to be in danger, Luna," he said with more force than he'd anticipated. The idea of her hurt or scared terrified him.

"Even if I'm surrounded by guards? And you could teach me, right?"

He shook his head. "No. I don't have time to teach you. I have too much to do." And with that, he took her hand and lifted her out of the seat. "And on the top of my priority list right now is making love to my wife," he told her.

Luna was about to correct him, to tell him that didn't make love, they had sex, but his mouth covered hers before she could say another word. And after that, she couldn't really say much at all. Dassar was the kind of lover that overwhelmed with passion, not leaving too much to rational thought. All she could think about when he started touching her was to find that fulfillment while, at the same time, drive him as crazy with need as he was making her.

# Chapter 11

"Good morning, Your Highness," Reyna called out from the edge of the bed with a cheery voice.

Luna's eyes slanted open, not sure if it was a good morning or not. "Give me time," she mumbled.

Reyna had a blue robe over her arm this morning and a cup of tea already steaming in her other hand. "Do you know what you'd like to wear tonight?" she asked, handing the cup to Luna and then holding out the robe so that Luna could slip her arms into the sleeves.

Luna knotted the tie of the robe while she padded into the bathroom. "Why do you need to know what I will be wearing tonight?" she asked, her eyes still not fully open and her mind was definitely not functioning at high capacity at the moment.

Reyna turned on the shower, adjusting the temperature. "So that we can match your nails to your outfit for tonight," she said as if that were the most obvious answer.

Luna groaned even while she sipped her tea. Stepping into the shower a moment later, she considered her options. She could spend another pointless day in the spa with all of the other ladies, or she could start to make her world better. She might not be able to convince Dassar to love her. She knew that. She also knew that her feelings for him were far and away stronger than she would have liked. And she was ready to live her life loving him completely. It would be a lonely life, but she could do it. Somehow, she could fill her life with things that made it okay.

When she stepped out of the shower, she took the towel that Reyna had already placed on the heater, drying herself off. When she stepped out of the bathroom, Reyna had yet another robe ready for her, probably in anticipation of spending the day in the spa areas. "Is there a gym?" she asked.

Reyna looked back at Luna with a blank expression.

"A gym," Luna clarified, "a place to exercise and work out?" she went on. "Is there a place like that in the palace?"

Reyna's eyes cleared up. "Of course! His Highness works out every morning!" And she went into the closet, coming back out moments later with a dress in each hand. "Would either of these work for tonight?"

Luna glanced at the dresses with exasperation. "Reyna, are there any clothes in there that would work for exercising?"

Reyna again looked at Luna with confusion. "Why would you want to exercise?"

Luna laughed softly. Obviously physical exertion for women was a foreign concept. "I'm not sure if I want to exercise so much as learn self-defense." She pulled out a pair of leggings and a tee-shirt. These were her old clothes and she had to sift through the drawers to find a sports bra. But when she found all the items, she was relieved and feeling much more comfortable. Coming out of the closet, she looked at Reyna. "Now I need to speak to the head of my security team. Who is that?"

Reyna opened her mouth, then closed it again. "Umar is the captain of your team, your highness. But I don't understand."

"Does Umar speak English?"

"Of course, Your Highness."

Luna sighed. "Reyna, would it be okay if you called me Luna instead of Your Highness?"

Reyna was horrified by such a suggestion. "Oh no, my lady! That would not be appropriate."

Luna grimaced. "I sort of thought that would be your answer. Okay, so back to the guard. Which one is Umar?"

"He is outside the doors now."

Luna opened the doors and looked at the two men who were standing sentry outside the doorway. "Umar?" she asked of both of them.

One man stepped forward after a slight hesitation. "Yes, Your Highness. How can I be of assistance?"

Luna smiled brightly. "I need to learn self-defense," she told him.

The man only stared back at her. "Excuse me?" he finally said.

"Self-defense. I need to learn it so that I can leave the palace when I need to."

The man stared blankly at her for another moment. "We are all here to protect you, Your Highness. We live to serve you and protect you."

Luna shook her head. "I appreciate that, but Dassar, or the sheik, or whatever I'm supposed to call my husband, said that if I wanted to leave the palace, I needed to learn self-defense. So if you would teach me, that would be great. If you can't, then perhaps you could recommend someone who could come to the palace and teach me?"

He bowed, finally understanding her request. "I would be honored to teach you anything you'd like to learn."

"Great!" she said, clapping her hands together. "So can we start now?"

The man still looked confused. "What kind of self-defense do you want to learn?"

It was Luna's turn to look confused. "I'm not sure. What would you recommend? I need to be able to fight off anyone that could break through your defenses. Does that help?" She saw the affronted look on his features and held up her hands. "I sincerely doubt that anyone will break through your defenses, Umar. I've seen the way you guys work and it's very reassuring. But Dassar won't let me leave the palace unless I can defend myself. So…what can you teach me? Hand to hand combat? Karate? Or is there something that would be better if someone were to try and kidnap me?"

The man seemed to grow a foot taller at her compliment and dismissing tone when it came to Dassar's concerns. But he smiled slightly at her list of options. "Perhaps I could teach you some combinations for getting away from anyone who might dare to try and harm you."

Luna was all for that. "Okay. Let's go."

Umar turned and led the way to the gym, even while he was calling in something through his radio. The three of them entered the gym which was huge, well equipped with every type of equipment she could imagine as well as a large matt area. It was to this area that Umar brought her. He'd taken off his jacket and his tie, instructing her to take off her shoes, just as he did, leaving them both on the matt.

And for the next two hours, he showed her various moves, even bringing the other guards into the lesson so that he could show her how to get out of a situation in which multiple attackers were trying to get to her. He made her practice each move over and over again until she did it perfectly and automatically.

By the end of the lesson, he bowed to her. "You are a very good student, Your Highness," he said.

Luna bowed to him as well. "And you are an excellent instructor!" she laughed. Turning to Reyna, who had been sitting on one of the stools during the lesson, she said, "Okay, I'm going to shower and then, would you show me to the kitchens? I don't know what I'd like to do next, but I do my best thinking in the kitchen while baking."

Reyna was more than happy to show her where the kitchen was and even argued with the head chef for space on one of the tables. For the rest of the afternoon, Luna baked one high carbohydrate delicacy after another, all the while, her mind sifting through the possibilities. She had no experience with finding a role for herself in a royal capacity, but she knew that she wanted to do something. The possibilities were endless, she thought.

But she needed to narrow it down to something that she loved doing. Something that she was passionate about. And also, something that could aid in bringing Altair back to the world stage economically.

Her hands pounded out the bread she was making after letting it rise for the past few hours. And then it hit her! Baking! What if she could translate her love of baking and her knowledge of sweets to the kids that needed some help? There were thousands of kids from broken homes that just needed guidance. Baking always helped her work through problems and it could also be a good vocation. Why couldn't she teach kids to bake? She had dozens of recipes that she could teach them!

Over the next week, she worked on her problem. In the mornings, she worked out with Umar and developed her self-defense skills and in the afternoon, she worked on her idea for a baking school. She wrote down her recipes, foods that were always in her head but she just baked them from memory or from the way Jeanie and Debbie used to teach her to bake. When she was finished with those, testing them she brought them to the chef. He was irritated with her initially, but when she explained what she was trying to do, he listened with more attention. Eventually, the two of them were leaning over the counter and brainstorming about possibilities, adding to the recipes, the chef giving her advice on how to simplify some of her recipes, or make them more complex by adding spices or herbs. Luna was fascinated with his expertise and laughed as they worked their way through a plan.

A week after their wedding, Luna was thrilled that she might have a plan that she could present to Dassar. So when she stood in the dining room, waiting for him that night, she had plans and layouts all ready for him to review. All she needed was his permission to travel outside of the palace to see if this kind of a plan would fit.

It suddenly occurred to her that she hadn't been outside of the palace since she'd flown into the country. And that hurt. She tried to pretend that it didn't, but why was he keeping her under wraps? Why was he hiding her away?

Then the memory came back to her. After his initial proposal, he'd told her flat out that he would not love her.

Since she was madly in love with the man, her heart ached that those feelings would never be returned. Every night, he took her into his arms and…had sex with her, showing her so much and giving her pleasure she could never have imagined before meeting Dassar. But….

She pushed that aside and walked to Dassar's office, eager to present her idea to him.

"Is he available?" she asked Hasif when he stood up.

"For you, of course," Hasif said with a bow.

Luna walked into Dassar's office and found him sitting behind a massive oak desk with papers spread out across the top. He looked to be concentrating hard on something but when she stepped through the doorway, did his face brighten?

"Luna!" and he stood up, coming around his desk to greet her. "What are you doing here?"

Luna gripped the papers in her hands nervously. "I have an idea for you. I wanted to see what you thought of it."

He kept her hand in his as he led her over to a sitting area. "An idea?"

Luna was once again nervous. He was so powerful and he had to deal with so many issues, her training bakery seemed silly now. "I don't want to disturb you. It looks like you're busy."

"Nonsense. I'd like to hear your idea."

She looked up into his dark eyes and melted, just like she did every time she looked at him. Goodness, he was handsome.

"Well, I was thinking that..." and she went on to explain her training bakery, explaining the recipes, the idea and the motivation behind the concept.

As she spoke, he took her papers, going through them and never once did he laugh at any of her ideas. He asked her questions and, in the end, he offered additional ideas. "This is good," he told her, his eyes focusing as he went back and forth with the papers. "A vocational school is a good idea."

Luna's heart soared! He liked her idea?

"I'd like to expand it a bit more though. Not just to baking but to other vocations, so that students have a choice."

She thought that was an outstanding idea! "Well..."

"I'll give this to Hasif and he'll find a place for the building." He stood up and took her hands, lifting her up into his arms. "Excellent idea, my dear. Thank you for thinking of this." And with that, he kissed her, making her whole body quiver with excitement.

There was a knock on the door and both of them turned to see Hasif opening the door. "I'm sorry to interrupt, but the prime minister is here to speak with you," he said.

Dassar squeezed her slightly. "Fine," he replied but with obvious regret in his voice.

"I have to go but thank you for this idea." He kissed her on top of her head and walked out of his office, handing the papers to Hasif before disappearing.

The rest of the afternoon, she had plenty of time to work up a righteous fury over their meeting. How dare he take her idea away from her! Why would he hand her idea over to Hasif? Why couldn't he let her work through the details? Granted, she didn't know all of the issues that would have to be worked out, but still....

She paced back and forth, furious that he wasn't letting her take over her idea.

And she was lonely, she realized as she stared at the still empty doorway while she waited for Dassar. She didn't speak the language well enough yet so Dassar's family generally kept away from her. Besides, they preferred spending their days in the spa and getting beauty treatments while she wanted to work, to contribute. She wanted to feel needed!

And she wanted Dassar to love her!

Oh, goodness, she thought as she sank down into the dining room chair, her papers and ideas under her hands as she realized that she would never have what she really wanted.

When he stepped into the room, she turned to face him. Her mind was so wrapped up in her thoughts that she actually forgot about her idea for a training bakery. "Are you ashamed of me?" she asked before he could even close the door to the dining room.

Dassar was startled by her words. His eyes traveled up and down her figure, noting that she was wearing a soft, pink dress in figure hugging material that made him want to carry her back to their bedroom and make love to her for the rest of the night. Forget food. All he needed was Luna in his arms.

"I am not ashamed of you. Why would you ask, or even think, something like that?" He moved closer, enjoying the smell of her femininity. "You're a beautiful, vibrant woman and I'm proud to have you as my wife."

She sighed, trying to be rational. "Then why am I stuck here in the palace every day? I thought you wanted me to go out into the countryside and see how I could help your people."

"You do so much, just by being here."

Which she translated to mean that he wanted her here to produce a baby. "That's all I am to you, aren't I?" she asked, fighting back the tears that threatened. She should not be surprised, she admonished herself. He'd told her all of this at the beginning. He'd never lied to her. He'd been brutally honest and, if she had gotten the wrong ideas into her head, well, shame on her!

The idea that he had somehow hurt her, even inadvertently, tore into something inside of him. "What are you talking about? You're my wife," he told her with emphasis.

Her soft, blue eyes looked up into his darker gaze. "And what does that mean?" she asked softly.

His teeth ground together and his mind tried to understand what was going on. He didn't like these questions. He'd been perfectly happy with their arrangement over the past week. Why was she asking these questions? "That means that I protect you." And he enjoyed seeing her at the end of the day, he thought. He didn't say that. Nor did he mention that the idea of her smile distracted him during the day and that he constantly wondered what she might be doing. He received reports that she was doing something in the kitchens and working out, but what else?

He mentally chided himself. He didn't need to know what she was doing. She was his wife, that was all. When she became pregnant, he would cherish their children but nothing more.

Luna saw the hard look in his eyes and it hurt. She shook her head. "That's not what a marriage means to me. And let's face it, you married me only to fulfill the terms of that horrible treaty."

He shook his head, fighting something deep in his gut that was clenching, twisting with the idea that she might be hurt. "You're wrong."

She looked up at him. "Really? So why did you marry me? Why did you pick me out of all the women you could have chosen and lift me out of my happy life only to lead me to this," she said, lifting her arms as if to encompass the whole palace. The files she'd wanted to discuss with him again dropped out of her arms and onto the floor but she didn't care. "I want more, Dassar. And I don't know how to get it. So I need to know if there is any way you could stop this marriage and find someone else." Goodness, where had that come from? And did she really want that? Did she want to be away from Dassar?

She wasn't sure what she wanted other than his love. Yes, that was the biggest priority in her life but would she get it? She looked up into his furious eyes and cringed. Probably not. The man was possessive, but other than that, she didn't think he felt anything towards her. Lust. Yep, lust was on that list.

Oh, goodness, was she simply not lovable? Her father certainly hadn't loved her but she'd thought she'd gotten over that! Oh, what a mess! She'd turned a simple discussion about a baking school into a request for a divorce. She was nuts!

His eyes flared with fury and her words. "Absolutely not." He would not let her leave him! She was his wife! She was his beautiful woman and had been from the moment he'd laid eyes on her.

She wiped at the tears flowing freely now. She couldn't stop them. "I know that it will be hard but since no one has really seen me outside of the palace, then maybe you could simply substitute another woman for me."

He was livid that she would suggest something like that. She was his wife, not some female that could be switched out at random. "What? The life of luxury is not good enough for you? The life of a woman who can do whatever she wants?"

She stepped back, wanting to hurt him just like he was hurting her. But he didn't even realize how he was wounding her with his words. "Dassar, I don't want a life of luxury! I want to be needed. Not just my uterus. I want my mind and my heart to be needed. You don't need those things. You just need an heir."

"So you're proposing to leave our marriage simply because you're not getting what you want?" He grabbed her upper arms and pulled her closer, his body rebelling against the idea of her not being curled up in his arms every night, of her not having dinner with him every evening and sharing her funny stories or listening to him talk about the issues of state. And that was quite a shock, he discovered. He liked talking…with a woman?

She pulled back, not sure what she was proposing, only knowing that she was sad and aching. "Dassar, you come to dinner every night and after we eat, you make love to me. But is it really making love?"

How could she even question that? "Yes! You are right there with me. Don't you dare deny what we have in bed together!"

She sighed and laid her open hand against his chest, trying to figure out what was really going on inside of her head. "You're right. We have something incredible in bed. And I don't know if any other man could give that to me."

He pulled her harder against his body. "You don't need to find out," he snapped, furious that she would even imply that another man could touch her. "I will give you what you need."

She looked up at him, her blue eyes pleading with him. "Will you love me? Will you make me a partner in this marriage? You saw a picture of me and came to Virginia. You blackmailed me into marriage and saved my adopted town, but do you really know me? Do you love me the way I deserve to be loved?"

He hated her words and, what's worse, he hated that her words made his chest ache. "Love is not necessary for this marriage to work," he snapped, ignoring that ache.

She laid her head against his chest, hearing his heavy heart rate. "Love is necessary for every marriage to work."

"You're suggesting that you need something else!"

She gasped at his obtuse statement. "Of course I want something else! I want you to love me!"

"I don't do love, Luna. I told you that from the beginning."

She hurt. Deep down inside, she hurt as she'd never been hurt before. "I see," she whispered.

But she didn't see. She didn't understand. And right at this moment, he knew that he needed to get her to understand so that she would cease this ridiculous talk of switching out another woman to take her place. "Love is what got four countries into a ten year war. Love makes a man weak."

Luna looked at him with hurt, wounded eyes. "I won't make you weak, Dassar. Love makes people stronger. Love unites people and gets them through the hard times." She looked up at him. "Like now." Gently, she pulled her arms out of his hands and stepped back.

And she walked out of the dining room. She vaguely heard Dassar calling for her but she ignored him. This was it, she thought. This was her life and she really didn't like it but she had no idea how to fix it. She'd thought that finding a goal, a project would help her. But in the end, she realized that she really needed Dassar's love, something she'd never have.

She should have controlled her emotions better. She should have ensured that she didn't get hurt by falling in love with a man like Dassar. And if he'd just left her in her little town, she would have been fine.

Okay, so she wouldn't have ever known the beauty of Dassar's touch or the magic of being in his arms.

As she hurried down the palace hallway, not really even knowing where she was going, she told herself that this was all her fault. He'd warned her from the beginning that he didn't do love. He'd explained the terms of this relationship. He would take care of her and give her anything that her heart desired. Just not love.

But what if all she wanted was his love? What if being with him didn't make sense if he wasn't emotionally connected with her?

She didn't know. She found an empty room and slammed the doors. It was dark in here so she didn't know what the room was used for. And it wasn't like she could really hide. Her guards were right outside the door. They would tell Dassar where she'd gone.

Not that he would care.

She curled up in one of the chairs, hugging her arms around her and trying to stop the crying. She hated crying! It was pointless and silly. Tears solved nothing and simply obscured problems instead of solving them.

She wiped angrily at her cheeks, not wanting any evidence of such a weakness. And as she stared out at the moonlight, she tried to think of what she would do. How was she to handle this kind of a relationship?

She didn't have an answer. She'd been silly to tell Dassar to find another woman but what else could she say?

Her hand covered her stomach as another thought hit her. What if she was already pregnant? He never used any sort of protection. And coming up with contraception hadn't occurred to her either. Not that she would have been able to do it. He'd sort of swept her off of her feet from the moment he'd walked into her inn until now.

She wiped her tears and, as her eyes adjusted to the dim light, she walked over to a sofa, curling up on one end. She wondered what this room was used for. There were so many rooms in the palace, all of the furnished beautifully, but many weren't ever used.

A bit like her love, she thought. It was there, right in front of him, but he didn't want it.

A sudden thought hit her. Maybe he did want her love, but he couldn't admit it. Was that possible? She had no idea. It was silly, but she didn't know Dassar well enough to understand what motivated him.

But maybe the history of Altair was the answer. The war had started a bit more than ten years ago, but what had precipitated hostilities? She remembered something about long ago weddings, but how in the world could weddings cause violence? It didn't make much sense.

Nothing made a whole lot of sense to her right now, she realized. And she was exhausted. She wasn't sleeping as much as she should, but that had always been okay because Dassar's lovemaking made her feel more alive. By this point in the evening, she would already be in his arms, gasping for breath as he made her body hum with excitement.

She laid her head on a pillow, just staring out the window as the moon slowly rose over the palace. Luna sighed with confusion and heartache. She was silly, she told herself. She couldn't leave Dassar. He'd never love her, not the way she loved him. What was she to do?

Dassar walked into the dark room and found her asleep on the sofa. She didn't look comfortable at all. With grim determination, he lifted her into his arms and carried her back to their suite. There was no way he was going to sleep without her. He hadn't ever slept with a woman before her, but he'd gotten used to her so she could just damn well sleep in his arms from now on!

As he laid her down on their bed, he was surprised that she didn't even stir. He slipped her shoes and slacks off, then stripped down to nothing before slipping into bed beside her. His body was already hard and aching for her, but he wouldn't make love to her. Not tonight. They would talk tomorrow and he would figure out a way to make her happy. She'd damn well be happy too, he said in his mind! He'd read the background report on his lovely Luna and Dassar wished that her father was still alive. Dassar severely wanted to hurt the man for what had happened to Luna while in the man's care.

She mumbled something in her sleep and snuggled against him. Dassar stared up at the ceiling, his mind forcing his hands to not move, to not pull her into his arms so that he could make love to her. She was exhausted and needed sleep.

# Chapter 12

Luna woke up feeling warm and more comfortable than she could ever remember being. And she felt wonderful after a full night's sleep. Dassar was amazing in bed, but he didn't let her sleep very much.

As she yawned and moved closer to the heat source, she wondered where Reyna was. Normally, she was standing by the bed with her tea all ready.

When that heat source moved, she was startled awake. A split second later, she was on her back with her arms up over her head with a very angry, very determined Dassar staring down at her.

"What are you still doing here?" she asked, trying to get her hands out from his grasp.

"You are not leaving me, Luna," he told her firmly, ignoring her question.

She blinked, but wasn't sure how to respond. "I know that," she finally said. She noticed his shoulders relax slightly after those words. And then she dared to ask the question uppermost on her mind. "Why do you care?" She held her breath as she watched the emotions rush across his handsome features.

In the end, his answer was less than she'd hoped for. "Because you're mine," he replied and bent lower to nibble on her neck.

She gasped when she felt his teeth against her skin and shifted when he pressed his legs between her knees. No, she thought as his hands released her wrists, she couldn't leave this man. She'd spoken in anger and desperation last night, feelings she hadn't even thought were on the periphery of her mind.

His mouth covered hers, sending her to that place where her mind stopped functioning. "And you love me," he told her. He didn't give her a chance to respond. His body invaded hers and she gasped as she lifted her hips to try and accommodate him better.

"I've never said that I love you," she gasped out.

He moved inside her tight sheath, shaking his head so that he didn't lose control like he normally did when he was in this position. "You didn't have to say the words," he growled, his hand moving into her hair, his fingers tangling with those platinum tresses. "You couldn't be like this with me if you didn't love me."

105

He was right, she thought and let her hands move lower so that she was gripping his hips. "Okay, I love you!" With those words, he gave her everything she could hope for. Pressing himself into her, he shifted and moved so that he gave her maximum pleasure. And when she screamed out her release, she said the words again, unaware that they triggered his own climax. All she knew was that she had to hold onto him. Never give him up!

A long time later, she stirred enough to realize that he had pulled her back against his chest, the entire back of her body plastered against the front of him and she sighed with contentment. "I have to shower," she told him and slipped out of the bed.

He watched her walk to the bathroom, amused that she was still shy around him and had taken the sheets to cover herself up.

Dassar leaned back against the pillows, thinking that the issue was finally resolved. But his lovely wife turned and looked back at him, looking saucy and enticing with the sheet falling down her back. "But if you've come to the conclusion that I love you based on my actions and the way I react to you, then…" she smiled and his body hardened once more, "you're madly in love with me too." With that, she dropped the sheet and walked into the bathroom naked.

Dassar vaguely heard the shower running but it wasn't at the forefront of his consciousness. His mind was completely focused on her words. It was as if he'd just been shot in the chest or punched in the gut. He could barely breathe for a long moment as he tossed those words over and over in his mind.

When he finally reacted, he jumped out of the bed, livid at her for even suggesting that he was in love with her.

"I am not in love with you, Luna!" he roared, standing in the opening of the shower.

Luna spun around, her hands soapy and a startled expression in her eyes. She looked up at him, then down, noticing his erection but pushing it out of her mind. At least for the moment. When she noticed how angry he was, her heart soared! If he wasn't in love with her, he would have come in here and, possibly made love to her again, but he wouldn't be so furious. She suspected he would be condescending or objective, but he wouldn't look like he was about to explode.

"Of course not," she replied and smiled as she turned back around, rinsing the soap off of her body. "Silly me. What was I thinking?" she teased.

Dassar watched her, trying very hard to ignore the bubbles that were flowing down her delicate figure. He wanted to lift her up into his arms and shake her for saying something so outrageous. "I will not love you, Luna! That was the understanding from the beginning."

She laughed softly as she nodded her head. "Yes. You're right. You did warn me of that." Even as she said the words, her heart soared with happiness. Dassar loved her! He really, really loved her! Oh, goodness, she couldn't believe how that revelation made her feel.

"You're just going to have to get used to the idea that I won't ever love you, Luna," he told her, his hands fisting on his hips. His eyes watched with fascination as she massaged shampoo into her hair. Was she teasing him? The laughter in her eyes told him that something was going on inside her pretty head but he couldn't figure it out. Not with the way his body was throbbing and his head was pounding.

He stepped into the shower, pushing her hands out of the way and taking over the task himself. Dassar felt her lean against him and he moved one hand down around her waist, pulling her more thoroughly against his erection and the rest of his body. "You're too soft," he told her. His hands were thoroughly washing her hair. "And you're too tender. I told myself I shouldn't marry you, that I should choose another woman."

She leaned her head into the water, rinsing out the shampoo. "But you didn't," she said. She turned around and lifted the soap into her hands. "You married me." She kissed the middle of his chest. "And you fell in love with me." Her hands wrapped around his erection, effectively stopping any arguments he might make with her statement. His arms reached out, bracing against the sides of the shower walls.

When she went down on her knees and took him into her mouth, his head dropped backwards and she could feel the tension vibrating in his enormous body. She didn't let up on her ministrations, giving as good as he gave to her. Unfortunately, he only allowed her a few minutes of that pleasure before he grabbed her and lifted her into his arms. Bracing her against the wall of the shower, he entered her, hard! She gasped and shifted, then smiled into his passionate eyes. "I love you," she whispered. Leaning forward, she wrapped her arms around his neck and bit his ear. "I love you!"

He shook his head but Luna knew with every feminine instinct inside of her that he was shaking his head at his own feelings, not denying what she felt for him. She kept whispering things to him, how much she loved the way he touched her, the way he felt when he was inside of her and how she missed him during the day. The whole time, she gently absorbed his thrusts, taking everything he was willing to give her.

In the end, he took her higher than ever before and she had to stop whispering to him since she was screaming out her release. She wasn't even sure what happened to him. All she knew was that she was complete and he was holding her. That's all she needed because, deep down, he loved her.

Dassar couldn't believe what had just happened. He'd been too rough, too hard on her! He berated himself until he pulled away and looked down at her. When he saw the look of ecstasy on her lovely features, something cracked inside him. "Are you okay?" he asked, his voice rough. He set her down on the shower floor and held her steady until he was sure she could stand.

"I'm more than okay," she laughed, still leaning against the marble of the shower wall. "Thank you," and she leaned forward, kissing his arm because he'd turned back to dip his head under the water.

She walked to the opening and grabbed a towel, drying herself off as she watched him. His arms were once against spread out, bracing against the walls of the shower but he wasn't moving, just letting the shower spray pelt against his head.

She was almost dry when he spun around, his eyes once more angry. "Dammit Luna! I don't love you!"

She was startled for only a moment until she saw the vulnerability in his normally hard eyes. "Yes. You do." And she held his gaze for a long moment.

He smacked the water off, then walked over and grabbed another towel. He dried off quickly, then wrapped the towel around his waist. "You're…." he started to say something but stopped himself. Shaking his head, he walked by her, leaving her alone in the bathroom.

Luna smiled but hid her expression in another towel as she followed him out of the bathroom. She expected to find him in his dressing room pulling on clothes but instead, he was pacing back and forth across the bedroom. His hair was messed up and his shoulders tense as he worked through everything in his mind.

When he caught her, he glared. "You don't understand! Love is what caused four countries to start a ten year war." He pointed out through one of the large windows. "I will not do that to my people again."

She suppressed the amusement that bubbled up inside of her. "I know that, love. I would never ask you to start a war over me. I promise." She shrugged in the towel. "Besides, I don't really have a country of my own. So there really isn't anyone who would fight for me."

His eyes were on fire. "That's the problem," he told her grimly.

His hands raked through his hair again. And then again. Back and forth he walked and Luna had no idea what was wrong. "Could you explain that to me?" she asked softly.

He glanced at her, then away. With a sigh, he stopped, going over things in his mind. When he leaned his head back, staring up at the ceiling, she wondered if he'd come to some sort of conclusion.

Then he walked over to her. Looking down into her blue eyes, Dassar was clenching his teeth as he admitted, "I would fight for you, Luna."

Those words, spoken with such intensity, thrilled her heart more than anything that she'd ever heard. But she also recognized the problem they created within him. Lifting her hand, she cupped his rough cheek. "Dassar, you don't need to fight for me. I'm right here. I'm not going anywhere."

He leaned his head into her touch. "That's not what you said last night," he argued.

She stepped closer to him, leaning her body against him and smiling when she felt his arms wrap around her. "I was wrong. I said things last night because I was confused and I wasn't sure how to deal with what was spinning around in my mind. But I shouldn't have said those things. I was so wrong and I'm sorry." She looked up at him. "I won't ever leave you. I love you," she told him urgently.

His fingers dove into her wet hair, pulling her hard against him. "I can't love you," he argued. "It isn't good for my people."

She laughed. "It is great for your people," she came right back. "You want them to be happy. You want them to thrive. And love helps them to do both. Without love in the world, wars will start up and people will be miserable."

He groaned. "I knew you were too much of a romantic," he told her.

She smiled. "But you love me anyway."

He pulled away from her, kissing her gently. "I don't want to love you."

"But you do. And I love you."

He sighed, leaning his forehead against hers. "Yes." He closed his eyes with that admission.

Her arms tightened around his waist and she almost started crying again. "I love you so much. And I promise it won't hurt."

He laughed. "I think I used those words on you at one point."

She smiled happily as her eyes misted up. "Yes. But this is so much better."

"I love you," he finally admitted. "I didn't want to. But now that you've gotten to me, you're going to be in so much trouble. Because I'm going to love you more than you could ever imagine."

She sobbed with happiness. "Promise?" she whispered through her tears.

"Promise."

# Excerpt from The Sheik's Convenient Bride, Book 6 in The War, Love, and Harmony Series

"Anything else on the agenda?" Tarek called out, relieved that this meeting was finally coming to an end. It was a monthly meeting with his cabinet members. All of them trying to show how important they were to his government and all trying to push him to do one thing or another.

"There's just one other item," Yousef called out, already looking uncomfortable with the next topic.

Tarek looked down. There was nothing else noted on the printed agenda. What could the man possibly want to discuss? And then he knew. His irritation increased as he looked around the table. Everyone wanted to discuss the same thing yet Yousef was the only one with enough courage to bring the subject up.

Tarek knew that he was the last one. The last of the four, the only holdout.

"My marriage," he stated blandly, leaning back in his leather chair at the head of the conference table. The peace treaty. Tarek sighed with irritation but knew that it had to be done. Marriage and an heir, ensuring the line and ensuring peace, he thought with resignation. He knew it was the best way, but that didn't mean he had to like it. But even he admitted it was time to produce an heir. He was thirty-five years old. Well past the age when he should be married with children. It was the right thing to do for the future prosperity of Tularia.

Leaning back in his chair, he tapped his gold pen against the papers in front of him, unconcerned that it showed his impatience. "It is going to be difficult to find a suitable candidate. The woman must be of Tulaurian ancestry. She must be young enough to be still able to conceive since the whole reason I'm doing this is to produce an heir," he stated firmly, looking around the table and daring anyone to disagree with him. "And she has to be old enough so she's not an irritating, simpering idiot." His eyes skimmed the table once more. "All of you have sons and lots of them," he called out with amusement. But then his eyes stopped on Ahmad, his interior minister. "Ahmad. You have a daughter." He remembered the girl from when she would run around the palace as a young child. "How old is she?" he asked.

Ahmad straightened suddenly, pride showing in his eyes. "She just turned twenty-four, Your Highness."

Tarek smiled as memories came back to him. Memories of his awkward daughter's somewhat ludicrous infatuation with him. "If I recall correctly, she stated very emphatically that she was either going to marry me or an orangutan. How is she doing with that goal?" he asked and everyone around the table chuckled as they recalled the incident. The woman hadn't been quiet with her childhood and adolescent crush.

Ahmad smiled fondly at that particular reminiscence as well. "She was just eight years old at the time, Your Highness. But as yet, she is not married." He straightened even more, pleasure showing in his demeanor. "In fact, she should be home from graduate school this afternoon. She is flying home for the summer before she returns to find a job."

A black eyebrow went up with that announcement. "Where has she been going to school?"

Ahmad's shoulders straightened even more. "She attended Stanford. Just graduated with honors with a master's of business administration."

Tarek closed his leather binder. "Bring her to the palace. She'll probably do." He stood up, shocking the rest of the group at the abrupt nature of their ruler's potential choice of a bride. "Have her come for dinner tonight."

With that, he walked out of the meeting room, his mind already ticking off the issue of his marriage as completed. Creating an heir shouldn't be too much a problem since he vaguely remembered the girl and she'd shown promise of being a beauty.

Ahmad watched his boss and ruler walk out, accepting the congratulations of the other members of the cabinet. Many were thinking that this was a huge boon to his career. All of them would have given their daughters to their ruler in marriage in a heart beat since that kind of a connection to the palace had incalculable advantages for one's future. But Ahmad had a different opinion.

His Kylie was young and beautiful, yes. The Sheik would have no issue with her soft, gentle beauty. But he suspected…no, he knew, that his precious and stubborn Kylie would not easily agree to such a union.

First of all, she'd had an embarrassing and very obvious crush on the sheik when she'd been younger. If it had been when she was four or five years old, his Kylie might be able to brush it off and move on with a smile. But she'd been twelve to Tarek's mid-twenties and she'd actually yelled at one of his dates to get her hands off of her future husband. The whole palace had been laughing about it for months. Her jealousy had become somewhat of a liability for her presence in the palace.

Secondly, his Kylie was not one to accept a superficial marriage. Despite her dedication to her studies and an adept, intelligent mind, at heart, she was a romantic. Deep down inside, she wanted the love and roses kind of marriage. Accepting a marriage from a man who had simply picked the most available woman from his cabinet members' family was going to increase her stubbornness to a whole new level.

He worried as he walked out of the conference room, not sure how to tell his lovely yet defiant daughter about this latest development. He still smiled at the congratulations from the other staff members as word spread, but this announcement would bring a whole new level of worry to his life. His Kylie was not a woman to be taken lightly. She was strong, opinionated, highly educated and had plans for her life, none of which included marrying her ruler. Ahmad knew that she'd planned to be here only for the summer and that was merely because he'd begged her to take a break and spend some time with him. She'd been pushing herself so hard lately, with studies and final exams not to mention that internship at the brokerage firm that she'd loved so much but which had taken up all the extra hours that weren't filled with studying. She would not appreciate the significance of this marriage, the honor it bestowed on whoever her ruler selected as his wife. In fact, he suspected that she would find it quite…

"Papa!" a sweet, familiar voice called out.

Ahmad looked around, his eyes widening with delight when he caught sight of his precious girl walking towards him. She was wearing a stern looking black suit that hugged her figure perfectly. The lines might be severe, but there was no way to hide her feminine figure, even with black crepe wool.

"What are you doing here?" he asked, taking her into his arms and kissing her cheeks. "I thought you weren't getting in until later this afternoon."

Kylie hugged her father excitedly, then linked her arms through her father's pretending like she wasn't blushing or anxious at being back in the palace after twelve, long, excruciating years. Now that she was back, standing in the hallway with everyone around her smiling and nodding their head in her direction, she suspected that all of her past foibles were going to be re-told once more in the private offices of each person here. Her plan had been to come and show the palace and cabinet members that she was no longer the stupid, silly little girl she'd once been, but she was realizing now that it would be harder to live down her past than she'd thought. An expensive suit and a sleek hair style wouldn't eradicate the memories of all her past antics towards their ruler.

Regardless, she told herself as she straightened her shoulders and walked with her head held high, she was only here for one month before she went back to California and started her job search. And she wouldn't have even come by the palace now if she hadn't had some silly notion of proving to the world that she wasn't still in love with Tarek, the big, bad ruler!

Darn it! She should have just stayed away, let sleeping dogs lie. Now she had to get through the long hallway, even walk past Tarek's office! What had she been thinking? It had been a foolish plan and all she wanted to do now was to get out of here and hide somewhere quiet, lick the old wounds that had never completely healed, and wish she could erase some people's memories of her past foibles.

"I don't want to disturb you, but I was wondering if maybe you had time for lunch?"

Ahmad was relieved to have an opportunity so quickly to bring up the subject and yet still tense, not sure how to bring up the reality that she'd probably been selected to be the next Queen of Tularia. How could he let her know without rousing that awesome stubbornness of hers? "Lunch would be wonderful, dear. In fact, I have plenty of time this afternoon for lunch and to hear about your finals," he lied. Ahmad actually had a packed afternoon of meetings and several reports to review. But he'd clear his schedule because this marriage was just too important. It needed to happen quickly and publicly, to let the people of Tularia know that the peace treaty that had been signed recently would last, that they could get their lives back together after the horrible war that had lasted way too long. "Let me just check in with my assistant and let him know. I'll be right back."

He touched her shoulder before moving off down the hallway towards his office. Kylie thought about going with him but really didn't want to run into anyone, thinking it was safer here in the dim hallway. There weren't as many people out here now that the meeting had dismissed so she could relax for a few moments while she waited for her father to return.

She'd thought it would be good for her, coming back to the palace to show everyone that she was a strong, successful woman, no longer the silly, childish teenager she'd been so long ago. But after seeing everyone leaving the conference room, staring at her with an odd smile on their faces, she knew that it had been the wrong idea. Her stomach clenched, knowing that they were all remembering her childhood blunders, probably recounting each of her efforts to gain Tarek's attention.

So instead of following her father down to his office, she preferred just standing here in the now-empty hallway and avoiding any further interactions with the palace staff who all seemed to have very long memories.

She leaned against one of the marble columns, taking out her phone and looking at the recent texts that had come in while she'd been on the plane. There were several from her friends and she smiled, laughing at some of their quips. Most of them had already started their job search and several had sent her messages giving her tips on what they're running into. Kylie made a mental note on some of them, laughed at others and shook her head at a few more.

Tarek came out of his office, intent on getting that report on the environmental study that should be finished. But he stopped cold, his eyes startled by the long, sexy legs in a pair of killer heels. As his eyes moved higher, he had to be impressed by the tight skirt that showed off the woman's heart shaped derriere. His eyes paused, enjoying the view for several long moments before moving higher. The woman had a tiny waist and hair that was swept up into an elegant twist, but several wisps had fallen out, adding a soft, romantic look to the woman's appearance.

This was the Kylie who had badgered him so many years ago? Where were the braces? Where were the braids and the androgynous jumpers? The child's body of years ago could not have revealed the figure that now graced his hallway and his eyes were astounded by the transformation. His own body instantly reacted to the curves and the…legs!

"You're more beautiful than your younger self prophesied," a deep voice said.

Kylie spun around, her eyes slamming straight into the eyes of the man she'd hoped never to see again in her life. Looking into those dark, intense eyes, every single crazy stunt she'd pulled, all of the silly exclamations she'd declared to whoever might be standing in the palace at the time, came rushing back to her. The little girl in her still remembered the painful crush she'd had on this man. And the woman couldn't believe the quickening of her heart rate as she looked up at him now.

No matter how hard she tried, she couldn't stop the blush that pinkened her cheeks and she quickly took a step backwards, trying to put some space between his extremely large, male body and her now-trembling one. He was so tall and standing way too close for her peace of mind. Of course, the length of a football field would be too close in her mind!

She couldn't see his eyes clearly because of the shadows cast by the overhead lights but she remembered them. They were a beautiful, dark brown and nothing, not even the dim light from the hallway could diminish his height or the amazing muscles underneath the tailored shirt he wore. He wasn't wearing a suit jacket which only meant that she could see the bulging muscles even better and her heart pitter pattered painfully before she could tell herself that she wasn't still infatuated with this man.

And unfortunately, fate had decided that she hadn't stacked up enough embarrassing moments where this man was concerned. The heels she'd chosen for today, the very shoes she'd selected to help her look more sophisticated and professional, the shoes she'd hoped would shift everyone's perception of her from a silly girl to a confident, strong and competent woman, backfired on her brutally. She was more used to sneakers and ballet flats as she hurried to classes or across the school campus. So backing up on suddenly trembling legs and four inch heels was not conducive to grace under pressure. Her heel tripped on some invisible obstacle behind her and she suddenly felt herself falling. No matter how hard she tried, her efforts to stop her fall, and avoid one more humiliating moment, only made it worse.

Strong hands reached out and grabbed her arms, pulling her forward instead of backwards and Kylie gasped when Tarek's hard chest pressed against her breasts.

"Careful," he cautioned with a strange, deep voice. "You have an important role now. We can't have you bruised before you venture out in public, can we?"

Out of the corner of his eye, Tarek caught Ahmad's imminent return and stepped back, his hands lingering on the slender arms of the stunning beauty standing stiffly in front of him. Kylie's father was still further down the hallway and couldn't see or hear the conversation, but Tarek knew that he would be heading this way any moment. He ignored her father's surprised expression at how close the two of them were standing and looked down into her pretty, hazel eyes. Yes, the decision had been made. This lovely woman would work out well for his purposes.

# List of Elizabeth Lennox Books

The Texas Tycoon's Temptation

**The Royal Cordova Trilogy**
Escaping a Royal Wedding
The Man's Outrageous Demands
Mistress to the Prince

**The Attracelli Family Series**
Never Dare a Tycoon
Falling For the Boss
Risky Negotiations
Proposal to Love
Love's Not Terrifying
Romantic Acquisition

The Billionaire's Terms: Prison or Passion
The Sheik's Love Child
The Sheik's Unfinished Business
The Greek Tycoon's Lover
The Sheik's Sensuous Trap
The Greek's Baby Bargain
The Italian's Bedroom Deal
The Billionaire's Gamble
The Tycoon's Seduction Plan
The Sheik's Rebellious Mistress
The Sheik's Missing Bride
Blackmailed by the Billionaire
The Billionaire's Runaway Bride
The Billionaire's Elusive Lover
The Intimate, Intricate Rescue

### The Sisterhood Trilogy
The Sheik's Virgin Lover
The Billionaire's Impulsive Lover
The Russian's Tender Lover
The Billionaire's Gentle Rescue

The Tycoon's Toddler Surprise
The Tycoon's Tender Triumph

### The Friends Forever Series
The Sheik's Mysterious Mistress
The Duke's Willful Wife
The Tycoon's Marriage Exchange

The Sheik's Secret Twins
The Russian's Furious Fiancée
The Tycoon's Misunderstood Bride

### Love By Accident Series
The Sheik's Pregnant Lover
The Sheik's Furious Bride
The Duke's Runaway Princess

The Russian's Pregnant Mistress

### The Lovers Exchange Series
The Earl's Outrageous Lover
The Tycoon's Resistant Lover

The Sheik's Reluctant Lover
The Spanish Tycoon's Temptress

### The Berutelli Escape
Resisting The Tycoon's Seduction
The Billionaire's Secretive Enchantress

### The Big Apple Brotherhood
The Billionaire's Pregnant Lover
The Sheik's Rediscovered Lover

The Tycoon's Defiant Southern Belle

The Sheik's Dangerous Lover (Novella)

**The Thorpe Brothers**
His Captive Lover
His Unexpected Lover
His Secretive Lover
His Challenging Lover

The Sheik's Defiant Fiancée (Novella)
The Prince's Resistant Lover (Novella)
The Tycoon's Make-Believe Fiancée (Novella)

**The Friendship Series**
The Billionaire's Masquerade
The Russian's Dangerous Game
The Sheik's Beautiful Intruder

**The Love and Danger Series – Romantic Mysteries**
Intimate Desires
Intimate Caresses
Intimate Secrets
Intimate Whispers

**The Alfieri Saga**
The Italian's Passionate Return (Novella)
Her Gentle Capture
His Reluctant Lover
Her Unexpected Admirer
Her Tender Tyrant
Releasing the Billionaire's Passion (Novella)
His Expectant Lover

The Sheik's Intimate Proposition (Novella)

**The Hart Sisters Trilogy**
The Billionaire's Secret Marriage
The Italian's Twin Surprise (USA Today™ Best Seller!)
The Forbidden Russian Lover (USA Today™ Best Seller!)

**The War, Love, and Harmony Series**
Fighting with the Infuriating Prince (Novella)
Dancing with the Dangerous Prince (Novella)
The Sheik's Secret Bride
The Sheik's Angry Bride
The Sheik's Blackmailed Bride
The Sheik's Convenient Bride

**The Boarding School Series – September 2015 to January 2016**
The Boarding School Series Introduction
The Greek's Forgotten Wife
The Duke's Blackmailed Bride
The Russian's Runaway Bride
The Sheik's Baby Surprise
The Tycoon's Captured Heart

www.ingramcontent.com/pod-product-compliance
Lightning Source LLC
Chambersburg PA
CBHW060639130626
46555CB00002B/880